I0575757

Content Note: Contains occasional mature language and themes appropriate for older teens.

Copyright © 2025 by Fay Masterson and Bellamy Young

Published in the United States by Charset Books, New York, New York

Cover design by Sienna Rose

PCN: 2025907222

ISBN: 979-8-9925596-0-6

All rights reserved. This is a work of fiction. Names, characters, places, and incidents either are the product of the authors imaginations or are used fictitiously, and any resemblance to actual persons, living or dead, businesses, companies, events or locales is entirely coincidental.

No part of this book may be reproduced in any form or by any electronic or mechanical means, including information storage and retrieval systems, without written permission from the author, except for the use of brief quotations in a book review.

For all the teenagers out there who feel a little different.

I think every technology ever invented has the potential to become both a tool and a weapon.

BRAD SMITH

CHAPTER 1

HESTER, 19

"Delivery for Hester Taylor."

"That's me."

"Voice recognition accepted."

Hester watches as the silver drone zooms to a stop two feet in front of her. The compartment below its camera eye opens and she grabs the delivery bag from Lou's deli. The drone flies up towards one of Atlas Hawkins's perfectly formed clouds in the sky. As it climbs, she can hear it say, "You have a great day! And remember, the future is Atlas!"

"It's a good day to get off this planet, that's for sure," Hester mumbles between mouthfuls of her PB&J on white. She rescues a strand of chestnut colored hair that was being consumed along with the sandwich and crosses the road. A bulbous glider truck hovering above the concrete narrowly misses her as it moves swiftly by. The sign on its iridescent surface reads, "Kellogg's Krickets protein bars keep you going all day!"

As Hester nears the Ice Cube, a glider bus from the local

high school pulls away from the parking lot. A group of teens step onto the moving sidewalk that leads into the building.

Hester sighs as she takes in the monochrome clothes the kids wear, the lack of jewelry or weird hairstyles. They barely interact with one another. Only the personalized biochip tattoos on their right cheeks reveal some idea of what is living under their muted exteriors.

The teens are ferried single file into the square glass building through the main entrance. Their biochips are scanned, causing them to illuminate briefly. A speaker can be heard saying:

"WELCOME TO THE CAMBRIDGE YOUTH CENTER. KEEP TWO FEET BETWEEN YOU AND NON-FAMILY MEMBERS. PRE HAWKNET HACKING MEANS JAIL TIME. PRESIDENT HAWKINS WILL ALWAYS PROTECT YOU."

After finishing her sandwich, Hester steps into the entrance to the left of the moving walkway. For a second, she worries again that the system will finally catch on this isn't a Hawkins-issued biochip. But her Sanskrit symbol illuminates as it is scanned, and she is permitted entry.

As Hester crosses the threshold, watched by cameras peppered all over the bright, airy space, she overhears two teen boys speaking in low tones.

"Man, I wish I could've seen how DC12 evolved. From chatbot to World War Three in under a year? That code must have been blinding," says the boy with blond hair and a slight lisp. His biochip is a tattoo of a wolf. He looks around nervously as he talks.

His black-haired friend, acne-ridden with wide-set eyes, replies, "Yeah, I thought it would be on a sanctioned page, but it's pre Hawknet, bro. We can't taste it."

"I can hack your biochips if you want?" Hester says. "You can download everything about it."

The boys look up at Hester, startled. The blond one instinctively takes a step back from her. "That's... er... that's OK. I don't feel like going to jail," he says.

"She's joking, char. No one can hack the bios," interrupts his friend. His biochip is the Red Sox B.

Hester shrugs. "Fine by me. But you're right: the code *was* blinding." She walks away from them and over to the corner of the room where there are four Lehmann interface stations placed side by side.

Hester never tires of the elegant design: a cerulean blue sculpture gleaming in the late afternoon sun. With no sharp edges, the computer terminal has a built-in seat that molds instantly to each user's body, allowing ultimate comfort.

Only Lehmann could create these.

These stations are normally used by teens for career planning with virtual guidance counselors, but Hester has another task for the terminal situated by the wall. She slides into the seat and feels it yield to her weight. As she sits, the solid blue panel in front of her becomes a translucent screen, waiting to be connected to a counselor. But that won't happen today.

After checking she isn't being watched by the other teens in the room, Hester pulls a small black disc out of her pocket, its surface glassy smooth. She places it on the small desktop below the screen and it instantly morphs into the same color as the terminal, making it look invisible.

Hester smiles. Knowing her connection is now shielded, she closes her eyes and links her biochip to the terminal.

She opens her eyes to see the words in her mind appearing on the translucent screen in front of her—

Marvin?

It only takes a few seconds for her question to be answered.

It's been two weeks since your last update. Explain yourself.
Change of plans. Lehmann was uncooperative. She thinks it's a ridiculous idea and that I will fail spectacularly.
That is unfortunate. We'll have to rethink this. Time to come home.
What? No, not yet, Marvin, please. I got a job! The first 19-year-old in 25 years to work for the US military!
What?! What are you talking about?
I'm the new AI programmer for Camp Constellation! I was referred to the Pentagon by Prof. Snelling at MIT. Aced my interview yesterday.
Hester, this was NOT part of the plan. I see now that sending you was a terrible error in judgment.
But I'll have access to multiple AIs there, including Lehmann's! Just give me a month, OK? I know it will work!

Hester waits for a response, panicked at the thought of having to go home now. For several seconds, there is nothing. She can feel her heart beating faster while she waits.

This isn't some school project, Hester. Do I need to remind you how important this is?
No, of course not, Marvin. But you know it has to be me. I can do this. Please?
Right now, you have permission to continue, but ONLY until I think of a better way. Understand?
Yes! Thank you!

Don't get too comfortable. How are you? Have you made any friends?
Friends? God, no! The kids here are just—

She glances around the room at the kids scattered about. None of them are slouching or falling asleep. They sit at desks ramrod straight, barely glancing at one another as they do their homework using their biochips. Not even a stolen yawn or suppressed giggle—it freaks her out more than she can describe.

Hester looks back at the screen: Marvin is gone. She picks up the black disc and stuffs it into the pocket of her gray jumpsuit.

She stands up and the translucent screen becomes solid again. Relieved she managed to win Marvin over, Hester lets out a long breath and walks to the exit. As she passes by the two boys she spoke to, she fights the urge to scream at them to wake the hell up and *do something, say something!* But she knows it's pointless.

"Peace out, Earthlings," she mumbles under her breath. In two days, Hester will be on a NASA ship heading to Mars, and for her it can't come soon enough.

CHAPTER 2

ASH, 20

Above the barren yard of the Iksan Detention Facility, large, uniform clouds waft by. Twice a day, the Hawkins plant nearby produces six oktas of cloud cover—just the right amount to ensure that Iksan has enough rain.

Watching them go, Ash Deung wonders if people are still impressed by how perfectly formed they are, or if anyone not incarcerated bothers to appreciate the sky anymore.

"Put your hand here," commands a hollow voice in Korean.

Ash does as he is told and places his hand inside the palm reader being held out by the AI prison guard. He tries very hard to stop his hand from shaking. This is a big day for him.

The ill-fitting prison suit hangs on his rangy body, and he has a rash on his neck from his last shave. Ash's biochip has been powered down, erasing all chance of him connecting to the outside world.

The Kim Corp Model 3 guard has a smooth black titanium shell, a little battered from age, but still imposing.

No attempt has been made to make it look human, its body more like an elongated skeleton.

Ash stares at the words appearing on the curved screen it has for a face:

Ash Deung, male, 20.

Domicile: 32 Muwang-ro gil, Iksan-si.

Charged with attempted murder.

Serving 7-year sentence. 1838 days completed.

Then Ash sees quick images of himself at fifteen on the screen being arrested outside his apartment building, then standing in front of the magistrates to receive his sentencing with his father by his side, and finally arriving at the detention facility. He tries hard not to remember the terror he felt back then, so apparent on his face in the playback.

"Processing complete."

"Am I free?" Ash asks the guard, trying to keep the hope tempered beneath the surface.

The guard doesn't respond. It turns and walks towards the front gate, the movements smooth and almost graceful. Ash stumbles over the uneven concrete as he follows and curses under his breath.

The gate appears to be floating. The perimeter of the facility is invisible, allowing unobstructed views of the industrial buildings beyond. Ash thinks this is almost worse than a high steel wall. Every day for five years, he has been allowed to see the world moving along without him.

As they get closer to the gate, Ash sees a Jadong Beoseu belonging to the facility glide a few feet above the road. Its bulbous silver body is seamless, molded from a single piece of engineered aluminum. The driverless bus comes to a stop in front of the gate and descends so it is level with the curb.

The gate of the facility opens just as the bus door lifts up and disappears into the roof.

Ash's stomach flips as his father steps off the bus.

I'm going home.

His father puts on the coat he has been carrying over his arm. It's not lost on Ash that the guard's mechanical joints are nimbler than his father's organic ones. Twenty years of cleaning the machines at the Hawkins plant has worn down his body to a shell.

Ha-Joon Deung finally looks up and sees Ash standing there. Ash can't help but feel a swell of relief. He wants to run to his father, but the guard is still standing between them.

"Father," he manages instead, nodding.

"My son. I am glad to see you well today," Ha-Joon replies.

"I am well, Father. It is a very good day," Ash says, finally allowing himself to smile. "We won."

Ha-Joon frowns. He looks to the guard and back to Ash. Then he closes his eyes, clasping his hands together.

Behind his father, Ash can now see more people get off the bus. He recognizes the parents of the other prisoners here.

The guard leaves them and moves back into the yard. Ash turns and sees the eleven other kids imprisoned here have lined up. The guard holds out the palm reader to the first kid in line.

Ash turns back to Ha-Joon. "Father? What is happening?"

"I-I'm sorry. I did everything I could. We lost the appeal."

Ash's throat tightens, the words ringing in his ears. "But what about all the evidence? Neighbors seeing what she did to me? The bruises? Broken arm?" Ash's voice begins to rise.

"It wasn't enough," his father replies, voice tight.

"Not enough? Didn't *Eemo* show them the photos? The night she found me in the alley?"

Ha-Joon stares at the floor. "Your aunt didn't show up at the hearing. I tried but I could not reach her," he says quietly.

Ash feels like he has been battered all over again. His head starts to spin and he fights to stay upright. Until today he hadn't let himself believe he could be released early. Allowing himself that brief moment of hope was the worst thing he could have done.

Ash's father starts to cry, robbing Ash of the permission to. "I failed you. Should have taken you away from her much sooner... I... I'm so sorry, son—"

"Why are you here?" Ash demands, his voice starting to harden. "If I'm not free then what is happening?"

Ha-Joon's face contorts further. "They didn't tell you?"

"Tell me what?" yells Ash. He is starting to come apart now, feeling the rage bubbling up.

"You're all leaving. This place is being shut down."

"What? Where are we going?"

Ha-Joon turns as some of the other parents begin to move further away. They avoid eye contact. He turns back to Ash. "Please calm down. Don't make this harder for yourself—"

"Just tell me where I'm going, old man!"

Ash's father looks nervously at the guard, which has spun its screen around at the commotion.

"Mars," Ha-Joon finally manages to get it out. "You are being sent to Camp Constellation to finish your sentence."

"No!" cries Ash. "No!"

"ASH DEUNG," the guard booms as Ash's rising blood pressure and heart rate register on its screen. "REGULATE YOUR BREATHING OR THERE WILL BE CONSEQUENCES."

But Ash can't hear anything except the white noise filling his mind. All he can think about is making it across the road and into the maze of the industrial park beyond. As if being yanked by an invisible string, he leaps past his father and runs in front of the bus.

"Ash, stop!" yells his father.

Ash can feel the blood pounding in his ears. His mouth is like sandpaper but he cannot stop running. He is almost hit by a glider cab but it brakes a few feet from him.

He's about to reach the other side of the road when a bolt of lightning shoots up his left leg. In agony, he cries out and goes down. The arms of his gray jumpsuit extend out two feet beyond his fingertips and force his hands behind his back as they clamp together.

He looks down at his left ankle. Beneath the surface of the skin a small red light flashes. Ash knows if he moves, he will be shocked again by his implant.

Stupid, stupid Babo!

This time he cannot stop the tears from coming. As Ash lies in the street, his father is comforted by one of the other parents. He can't look at Ash.

Of course he can't.

Ash knows now he will always be on his own. Can't trust anyone but himself.

As he is lifted off the curb by the guard, it starts to rain. Ash can hear the *plink, plink* sound as it ricochets off the AI's face.

The guard's screen says, *Six months added for attempted escape.*

CHAPTER 3

DREW, 17

Sitting on the thin plexiglass chair, Drew shifts in their seat. They wish they had not worn such a thick pair of wool trousers for the court appearance. It itches them in all the worst places.

They wince. But not because of the trousers. Drew hates that their mother is crying. The remnants of a crumpled wet tissue cling like dandruff to her somber-colored sari. Her jaw is clenching, and she keeps swallowing as if thirsty. It makes Drew want to grab for her hand, but she is just out of reach on the other side of Drew's father.

Colin Ryan is glaring at some invisible spot on the ultra-white floor. Drew can almost see the bottled fury oozing out of him. Drew thinks it's time he started wearing hats regularly to cover up the bald spot in the middle of his red crop of hair. Or just get the bloody hair transplant, for God's sake. Every other father Drew knows has done it.

On the other side of Drew is Angelo, their younger cousin. He is wedged in between Drew's aunt and her husband. Drew can't tell what is going through Angelo's mind, but they know it's not the humanities test he's missing right now while they're being sentenced for their crime.

Drew feels a hot stab of guilt in their stomach as they see beads of sweat on Angelo's forehead. His biochip, in the shape of a medieval sword, glistens from the moisture.

Tall since the womb, with intense dark eyes and a major resting bitch face, Drew tried to fit in as much as possible with the other kids at Wren Academy, but gave up when it was apparent that everyone in sixth form was just as miserable as Drew was. They spend most of their time alone writing, musing on death, or hanging out with Angelo.

Angelo is two years younger than Drew and thinks of Drew as his best friend. Drew doesn't know if Angelo is their best friend or not. The comfort of having someone hang on your every word can drown out any uncomfortable questions you might not want to ask yourself.

Drew tells themselves he's family—they have a duty to watch over him. And Angelo idolizes Drew, would follow them wherever they went.

Which apparently would now be to Mars.

"It gives me no pleasure to do this, but a drug offense hasn't occurred in Finchley in twenty-five years," the judge says in between sips of what could be tea, or vodka. Impossible to know.

As he drones on about how serious a crime it is, and on school grounds no less, Drew wants to take the chair they're sitting on and hurl it at the judge. Though he's just a 3D image being projected in front of them, it would be a tasty entry to write about in their journal.

The only thing that stops Drew in that moment is the fear that Angelo would be given a longer sentence. Drew couldn't care less if they were up on Mars for life. Anything is better than this pointless existence they're living in London in 2053.

He's probably sitting on his patio in the sunshine, his stupid poodles yapping at his feet, while he's dooming us to two years on Mars.

Drew wonders what the judge's day job is. So few crimes are committed now that he must have to make money some other way. Unless he's one of the few wealthy bastards left in London who helped Hawkins Corp take over the water supply.

Drew is tempted to try and sneak a gander at the judge's info via their biochip, but keeping their eyes closed for too long will no doubt be seen as insolence. They scratch at the black circle with three lines inside it—the Celtic symbol for "awakening"—and it buzzes at their touch, which Drew loves. They're trying hard not to freak out at the thought of it being powered down, losing all contact with their digital life.

The judge kept on.

"At the behest of Solicitor Markham here, I will grant Master De Luca the request his parents made yesterday. If the papers are filed at my office by ten a.m. tomorrow, then Master De Luca can have a Matercopy accompany him."

Well, that's something, thought Drew. No special requests from their solicitor, though. Drew has no intention of bringing anything with them except the standard pre-loaded e-reader now that biochip access will be denied. And some earplugs. And motion sickness tablets.

Drew knows it was wrong. They are bringing such shame on their parents, who work hard in their chemist's and keep their head down like everyone else in this dull country. But Drew can't help it—they feel a tinge of pure pleasure at knowing they finally did something wild, unexpected.

Drew's father jabs them in between their shoulders to

make Drew stand with the others. Drew furiously scratches at their thigh where the itch has now gathered a cluster of pins and needles around it—*brutal.*

The judge's pixelated image fades. So does Angelo and his parents, along with both of their solicitors, the chairs and desk. Everyone around Drew and their parents disappears, leaving only the stark, white living room of their semi-detached house solid and real around them.

"I need a drink," says Drew's father in his lilting Irish brogue.

Drew's mother wipes her eyes. "But it's Tuesday—"

"To hell with the regulation, Nihira." He barrels toward the kitchen to unlock the safe where his one bottle of whisky is kept. Drew looks at their mother, that gnawing feeling of guilt rising again in their throat.

She starts crying again. "Why did you do it, Drew?"

A million things rush through Drew's mind: because they are treated like a toddler, because they can't go anywhere without being watched, because when the echoing screams die down in Drew's mind, all they feel is numb.

Drew doesn't say any of these things. They step towards their mother and rest a hand on her shoulder. "I'm sorry, Mother. I don't know why I did it."

She pulls Drew into a hug, the fierceness catching them off guard. "Take care of Angelo. And for heaven's sake, do exactly as you're told up there. I need you back here safe and sound."

Drew pulls away. "Yes, Mother."

Before selling drugs, they *always* did exactly as they were told.

That's the problem.

. . .

Juni, 17

Struggling to keep it cool, Juni watches as Sho's hand inches closer to her side of the table. The gold ring on his pinkie finger glints in the light of the diner.

He's just going for the saltshaker.

But, instead, he keeps his hand resting on the table, tapping in time to the tempo change in the painfully bland music that echoes throughout Constellation.

Juni fights the impulse to just blurt out, *Come on, grab my hand already!*

She can't believe she teased her hair into a high ponytail before meeting Sho. This is *not* her usual style. She tried on three outfits on her athletic frame before just putting back on the yellow jumpsuit she has worn all day.

Sho moves his hand just another inch closer.

Shit, he's talking! She needs to concentrate. She raises her gaze to his face: wide-open brown eyes that seem endless; cute, short Afro; his golden biochip that looks like an abstract butterfly... *And that smile? OMG, it's too much.*

"... So, they're landing just now. Do you want to go see?"

"Huh?" Juni is totally lost.

"New degenerates, Juni," Sho prompts, showing that beautiful smile. Juni wonders how one person can change the energy in a whole room by just opening their mouth.

Juni nods. "Right. Sorry, I can't, I should be uptiming right now on a confusion matrix assignment for Eleni's class."

Sho's smile fades slightly, then he takes a bite of his Meteor Burger. Not knowing what else to do, Juni takes a sip of her milkshake, soothed by the creamy cool hit of sweetness.

The bright pink "1950s diner" sign on the wall behind Sho begins to flicker. Juni looks around at the boldly colored canteen, with its checkered floor, bright red booths and pink tube lights curving around the ceiling above the long counter. Two teens are behind it dressed in white uniforms, serving food to three other kids sitting on stools.

"This is a weird-looking place. Feels like it was designed by a two-year-old," she says, attempting humor.

Sho looks around. "I like it. We don't have anything like this in Bulawayo."

"Apparently we did, like, two hundred years ago or something. Though why they've recreated it here in a prison is beyond me." Juni shrugs.

"I guess a lot of things were better back then," replies Sho.

"Definitely more assaulting to the eye," deadpans Juni. Sho gives her a half-smile.

She's screwing this up, she knows it, but is so out of her depth here. Sho is the first guy she's liked. Like, *really* liked. Courting is pointless now. Juni dreads the moment she turns twenty-one and her father starts to pick out prospects for her. Her older sister had to endure eight mind-numbing dates before the matrimony algorithm finally got it right, though Juni's not so sure the marriage is all her sister makes it out to be.

An upside to Constellation is that the kids aren't forbidden from hanging out together during their downtime. The AI "Bob" units stationed at the doors don't appear to pick up on raging hormones. As evidenced by the number of two-person occupied tables in the diner, this is hook-up central.

The two male Bobs are utility AIs programmed on Constellation for guarding the teens, assisting the staff, and general tasks around the camp. To Juni, they look like adult facsimiles of every jock in high school she steered well clear of.

Feeling the touch of Sho's hand on hers, Juni jumps a

little. She looks up from her milkshake to find him suddenly very interested in the saltshaker. Eventually he looks up and, seeing her warm expression, his posture relaxes. He grins.

What is it about this guy?

Sho leans in closer. He touches the biochip on her right cheek with his index finger, making her blink furiously.

"That's pretty. What is it?" he asks.

"Uh... it's a one and a zero intersecting," she replies, shrugging a little.

Sho smiles. "Code? That's cool."

"Yours?" Juni asks, feeling the heat rising in her chest as their faces get closer.

"It's an Adinkra symbol—*Hye won Hye*. It means 'that which does not burn.'"

Juni wishes her cheeks didn't feel like they were burning as he stares at her. She really wants to kiss this guy right now.

"So... meet me here again tomorrow after therapy?" he asks.

"Sure," she replies, trying to keep her voice as casual as possible.

Then something catches her eye outside the window of the diner. She frowns. Beyond the latticed clear dome that houses the juvenile camp, a man is floating in the air above the uneven red landscape. He is wearing only a navy shirt and pants. For a split second, she is shocked he has no spacesuit on to protect himself from the Martian atmosphere, but then remembers it's a Bob.

Attached to the dome via a long tether, the AI unit is holding an electronic reader. Suddenly, a strong gust of red dust swirls the Bob around, but he is unfazed. He continues to take the reading as he is blown about like a balloon. As she watches this strange dance, the clear panels of the dome start to become opaque as the suspended water inside them purge the radiation they have absorbed. It will be five minutes before she can see the landscape again.

Sho jumps up, leaving Juni's hand buzzing a little when he lets go. "I gotta go. I hear there's a new AI genius on the ship who's going to work with Althea. She's only nineteen."

This makes Juni sit up straighter. "What? No way. That has to be bullshit."

"That's what I heard." Sho shrugs. "Sure you don't want to come?"

"Next time, OK?"

"For sure. You know how to find me," he says with a smile.

As he walks through the diner to the exit, Juni knows her father would *never* allow her to date a guy like Sho. This thought thrills her.

Being a hundred and forty million miles from Earth has some advantages.

She moves her unfinished milkshake aside and taps the silver wristband on her right hand. Projected in front of her is a small transparent screen floating in the air. The words "Juni Legrosse. Inmate #125" appear with a selection of options below it: *Classwork, Work Schedule, Therapy Schedule, Constellation Map.*

"Keyboard," Juni commands, and the screen expands to include a neon green holographic keyboard within arm's length of her. She brings it in closer.

Words and equations appear lightning fast as Juni's hands slide over the floating keyboard. Settling in to finish creating the curriculum for her teacher's class, Juni comes back to her comfort zone.

CHAPTER 4

DREW

"Welcome to Mars. We will be landing at Camp Constellation in fifteen minutes. Please make sure you have all your belongings and secure your suits and helmets when directed."

Drew catches the tail end of the ship's announcement as they stir from a long nap. They have no idea how long they've been asleep. They think it's been five days since the ship entered the Dyson sphere wormhole to get here, but they've lost track.

Their throat is dry and itchy. They debate whether to go to the bathroom before they land, but shudder at the thought of walking over again to the waste evacuator port on the wall. Everyone can see them hooking up their 3D-printed suit to it via the tube attached their left pant leg. Just so bloody embarrassing. They decide to hold it.

They stare out the wide convex-shaped window situated at the far end of the spaceship's holding deck where all the juvenile offenders have been kept for the journey.

The stars shine brighter than Drew could ever have imagined. They blanket the sky looking like cloud cover in every direction. As Drew stares out, they thought they would only feel relief at finally leaving their pointless life behind, but as the ship travels through the endless expanse of space, they wonder if it really was worth it. They fight an overwhelming urge to find a release hatch and jettison into the twinkling oblivion.

Shaking it off, they shift their attention back to the holding room and the eighteen other passengers—not including the four military-grade AI guards in the cabin. They hold no weapons, but Drew knows full well they could crush Drew's skull in three seconds if provoked.

Drew has gotten to know some of the kids stuck on NASA's *Intrepid One* with them, though mostly they've been reading and hanging out with Angelo. The girl called Hester intrigues them. She keeps her distance from the others and doesn't appear to need sleep. She has an old-fashioned laptop computer she spends most of her time on, which surprises Drew, as no one else is allowed an interface like that. They want to ask her but have to admit they're a little afraid of her. There's something about her energy that says, "I'm not interested in you and never will be."

Drew realizes they see themself in her.

They are bunking beneath this kid from South Korea who has major issues. They all do, but this guy has taken "asshole" to the next level. Pale, terse and emanating enough menace to choke the life out of any conversation, Ash is a real downer. Drew is mad at their stupid life, but Ash seems ready to take out as many of his fellow humans as possible given the opportunity.

"Did you know he poisoned his mother?"

Drew turns to Chance, the American girl lying on the

bunk opposite theirs. She has her feet at a ninety-degree angle and is pushing against the bottom of the bed above hers while she braids her platinum hair. Her biochip is in the shape of a Gucci logo. She nods in Ash's direction.

"Really?" asks Drew.

Chance nods. "One of the other kids from Korea told me. Happened five years ago. She survived but is gonna be sucking food through a straw forever."

Drew can't decide if she's for real. Chance seems like a kid who might say anything to be popular, but they have to admit —this is totally on point for Ash's personality.

"What did *you* do, then?" asks Drew. "What's your evil sin?"

Chance sits up and swivels to face them. She grins and clears her throat.

"There once was a loser named Atlas,

Whose penis, alas, was a no-go,

Unable to squirt, he turned into a jerk,

and now the whole world is a shitshow."

Drew's mouth drops open. "Oh, my God! That was *you*? Last I heard, that was tasted two million times on the pre-web!"

"Three. Three million," Chance replies, straightening her shoulders. But then her smile drops a little. "For that I get to spend twenty-two months up here."

"What? Just for that?" Drew is stunned by the severe sentence for a viral rhyme.

Chance tries to shrug it off, but Drew can see her eyes well up before she looks away. They search for words of comfort, but before they can speak the ship's computer cuts in.

"Attention: put on your helmets and type your four-digit pin into your space suit's console. Repeat: put on your helmets and type your four-digit pin into your space suit's console."

Drew and Chance get off their beds and cross to the other side of the deck. They sit in their assigned seats for take-off and landing as the other kids do the same.

Drew eases into the curved metallic-looking chair, picks up their 3D-printed helmet from under it and places it over their head. There is a small panel on the front of their suit with a keypad. They punch in a code and the visor lights up with text:

Camp Constellation, Pelios Mons, Mars. Founded September 2052 by the US Army and NASA.
Dome size: 15 acres. 10 acres of outside space.
Water source: 12-mile underground lake.
Hours of daylight: 12.33.
Dormitories: 16 - male, female, non-binary.
2 cafeterias. 8 staff members. 28 AI teachers and therapists.
100 AI Bob units.
Current juvenile population: 236, ages 14-20.

The fear Drew had been pushing away until now hits them hard. It all felt like an escape from the drudgery of life in Finchley, but now Drew realizes that they are stuck on this planet for the next two years with a bunch of other whackos like them. Earth is a terrible place right now, but is Mars going to be any better?

Two chairs down, Angelo is having his helmet put on by his Matercopy. Drew is impressed by the newest model—she looks exactly like Angelo's mother. Once she is finished with the helmet, the AI copy picks up Angelo's hand and places her other hand on top, sandwiching it between. It's a little awkward, but Drew can see their cousin is calmed by the gesture.

Drew catches Angelo's eye and gives him a thumbs-up. Angelo manages one in return, then quickly puts his hand down when he can see that, seated in front of Drew, Ash is giving him the finger. Angelo turns his head down to avoid eye contact with him.

Drew glares at Ash, who notices and leans forward. "He's a baby boy. You too? Gonna lose it without your mother?"

"I'm not a boy. Or a baby," replies Drew, knowing this won't end well, but feeling their blood boiling.

As Ash laughs, the little black dots on his powered-down biochip scrunch a little closer together. "Yeah, yeah. Not a boy or a girl. But still gonna cry like a baby when I crush your face."

Standing by the door, the AI guard takes two steps forwards. Seven feet tall and made of an ultra-flexible polymer aluminum casing, these military AI can move as nimbly as a human but twice as fast. They point a mechanical finger at Ash.

Ash sits back in his seat, staring straight ahead. The guard doesn't step back. Drew hates how relieved they feel knowing the guard is now monitoring Ash closely.

The ship announces once more—

"Attention: remain seated and fasten your safety harness. The ship is landing in five minutes. Do not move for the remainder of the journey. Once the ship has docked at the landing site, follow your visor for instructions. Do not deviate from the instructions for your own safety and that of those around you."

Outside the window, Drew can now see a jagged

mountain reaching out of the dusty red terrain that stretches in all directions. At the base is a huge dome.

Here we go, thinks Drew.

Rehab Camp awaits.

Althea Ellis, 50

As Captain Althea Ellis runs on the treadmill, she can almost feel a sliver of joy appearing from a long-dormant corner of her mind.

Now *that* is unusual.

Althea runs harder in the hope that she can catch the feeling before it disappears, as if the speed of her feet pounding on the belt is creating the bubble that keeps expanding.

Just then, the black wristband she is wearing beeps. Without thinking, she hops off the treadmill and pulls a pill case out of her shorts. She opens it and downs two crescent-shaped pills in between catching her breath.

In that moment, she knows something is off. She looks back at the treadmill, which is still displaying her run time, heart rate and calories burned. She had a need to hop back on a few seconds ago, but suddenly it's not that important anymore.

The treadmill, sensing her weight is no longer on it, times out and folds in on itself to become a quarter of the size. It glides into the wall, blending seamlessly into it.

"Althea?"

She turns to see her second-in-command, Max, standing in the doorway of the staff gym. The room is small with no windows, but big enough to accommodate the two multi-purpose machines designed to maintain peak fitness.

"*Intrepid* will be landing in fifteen minutes. Didn't you see the alert on your Intralink?" says Max.

Althea grabs her towel and wipes down her face. She looks down at her wristband. "I must have missed it." She walks over to a small cubicle in the corner and shuts the frosted glass door behind her.

"Sanitizing. Drying. Deodorizing." Althea mouths the words along with the cubicle as it announces the cleansing protocol. In a matter of seconds, she is clean and dry, along with her tank top and shorts. She steps out and pulls a black jumpsuit on over them.

"Wendy is almost finished with the halo for TIM," Max says as Althea zips up her suit.

"Great. When can we test it?"

They head out of the gym and into the corridor, walking fast so they aren't late for the new arrivals.

"She has to check the absorption rate and reconfigure the LEDs for the new room they're in, so maybe another day or so," Max replies.

"Let's hope we can do what the military couldn't."

Max doesn't respond. He checks his Intralink—the same wristband as Althea's.

"What?"

He gives her a look as if to say, *You don't want to hear this.*

"Don't edit yourself. What is it?" she prompts.

"I just don't know if we should be exposing the children in our care to this. What if they get ideas, Althea?"

"Such as?"

Max seems to be weighing his words. They are comfortable with each other, but there is still an obvious hierarchy. "If this can do what we think it can, I'm worried it will give them a false sense of freedom."

"The parameters are in place, Max. Just think of the potential ways it could heal trauma. We could change their lives forever. Isn't that what we're trying to do?"

"Yes. Within reason," Max replies.

As they make their way down the corridor to greet the incoming NASA ship, Althea hopes she is right about the TIM program. She can't bear the thought of telling Commander Roberts it was a costly mistake.

CHAPTER 5

HESTER

As Hester reads the instructions for the landing procedures on her visor screen, a tiny patch of bright pinpoints appear in the corner of her left eye. They begin to swirl around, looking like miniature fireflies.

Well, this is bad timing.

She takes a deep breath and closes her eyes. But when she opens them, the tiny points are now floating across the words on her visor, alighting gently on the digital letters and then flitting off again.

Hester glances around to see if the others notice that her visor now looks like it's lit from within, but thankfully no one is paying attention. She closes her eyes and beats out a fast rhythm on her chest with the fingers on her left hand. The tapping only lasts a few seconds before she opens her eyes.

The pinpoints have gone.

At that moment, the spaceship's powerful thrusters engage, and they descend vertically towards a large, flat landing pad a few hundred feet away from the edge of the dome.

Hester has kept her distance from the other passengers, save for a few words when necessary. That hasn't stopped her from betting on which kid is going to fall apart first. (Definitely the scrawny kid called Angelo.)

In a different time and place, she might have been friends with Drew. They don't seem needy or as skittish as the others. Their droll view of life back on Earth is amusing and she was impressed by the way they didn't back down when Ash taunted them earlier.

Chance fidgets endlessly in her chair. Hester can practically see the fear pulsing out of her as they get closer to landing. Most of them have been sentenced to serve time here for ridiculous reasons. Except Ash—*that* kid could do with a clean reset.

At least this sad crew of misfits did something to pierce the shroud that cloaks everyone back on Earth. She can respect them for that.

With a shudder, NASA *Intrepid* makes a surprisingly smooth touchdown. Hester is impressed with the tech on this ship, though they need to improve the ride through the Dyson sphere—several of the kids threw up in their suits going through the wormhole.

"Repressurizing ship. Adjusting air levels to Earth's atmosphere," the ship's computer announces.

Hester's visor lights up with the words. "Landing procedure complete. Please remove your helmet and await further instructions from the guards." Her safety harness is released and she presses a button on the side of the helmet to remove it. She struggles with it far more than she'd like, scowling at Ash, who laughs as she pulls it off. She can't wait to get off this ship and start working.

The guards motion for the prisoners to head towards the heavy sealed door. As they get closer, the panel next to it flashes green and the door slides upwards. One by one, the kids file into a long corridor made of smooth gray metal.

They are led to changing rooms and ordered to remove their space suits. On a steel bench, Hester finds a sealed package with her name on it and, once out of her suit, she pulls out a green US military jumpsuit with the name "Hester Taylor" stitched on the right breast pocket.

As she puts it on, Hester suddenly becomes aware of Chance's eyes on her. Chance and the other girls in the room are all wearing white jumpsuits. One by one they take in her military garb. Hester says nothing. She just smiles breezily and zips up her suit as she walks back into the corridor.

The reassembled teens are marched into a spacious cargo area at the end of the corridor. On one side there are two machines. With a cockpit on top and wider bodies beneath, they look like aluminum spiders with six wide wheels. Hester assumes they are used to cross the dusty terrain on this planet.

All kinds of equipment are stored along the walls on either side of the cargo area. Hester can see her duffel bag on a cart with the other luggage, and next to that is a utility cart with boxes of packaged food on it.

Directly in front of the group is a large hatch. One of the guards walks towards it and puts their palm onto a small computer terminal next to it. Slowly the hatch opens out and Hester can see the ship has been connected to a long tunnel.

Hester instantly recognizes the woman standing at the entrance to the tunnel as Captain Althea Ellis. She doesn't know the man, who looks to be in his mid-thirties.

Captain Ellis was present via the comms link between Constellation and the Pentagon during Hester's last interview for the position. It was clear from her probing questions that she was competent and smart, but if she's in the pocket of President Hawkins, Hester has no time for her.

For a moment, the cargo area is silent. The kids just stand there like frightened deer, awaiting their new fate.

Then Captain Ellis steps forward into the room and smiles. "Welcome to Constellation. We're glad you made it safely. I'm Captain Althea Ellis. This is First Lieutenant Max Landry, my right hand. Despite my position, I'm not one for formalities, so please, call me Althea."

The kids seem unsure. None of them respond until she walks up to Drew and puts out her hand.

Drew shakes it. "Uh, hello. I'm Drew Kapoor-Ryan."

"I know. It's nice to meet you." Althea then shakes the hand of all the kids in the room, speaking in a warm, friendly tone. The kids awkwardly respond, clearly confused by her open manner.

She finally arrives at Hester, giving her a firm shake. "You're here. Great. I know you must be tired—"

"I'm fine. All I did was sleep on this thing."

"Alright. Why don't you go with Max. He'll take you to your room and show you the ropes."

"When can I get into the lab?" says Hester.

Althea lets out a small laugh. "Anytime."

Hester grabs the one duffel with her name on it from the cart that has now been unlatched from the storage area, relieved to be getting away from this tableau of uncomfortable introductions.

"Wait!" says Chance. "You're working here? You're not one of us?"

Hester shrugs in response. "I'm sure I'll see you guys around. Don't act stupid." She points at Ash. "You especially."

Ash curses at her under his breath.

She walks towards the tunnel with Max, passing the other shocked passengers as she goes.

"I thought we weren't allowed to have jobs 'til we turned twenty-one?" Chance says to Drew.

"Oh, everyone has to work at Constellation, Chance. It's part of your journey towards healing," responds Althea, overhearing.

As Hester enters the tunnel, she sees a male AI Bob unit walking towards them. The Bob holds the arm of a sobbing girl with cropped, dark hair. A suitcase is rolling behind her on a small electronic trolley. Behind the trolley three boys and a girl follow along. Another female Bob completes the group, issued with a standard brown ponytail.

Althea turns at the sound of sobbing and walks back over to the tunnel. As she gets closer, the girl tries to calm herself, but struggles.

"Please, Althea," she pleads in a German accent. "Don't send me back. I hate it there! I want to stay!"

Althea hugs the girl and whispers something in her ear that Hester and the others can't hear. Althea places her hands on the girl's shoulders and she begins to calm down. The girl hangs her head but finally walks through the hatch unaided, not making eye contact with the others.

Althea is hugged goodbye by the four other teens who file in behind the German girl.

"OK! Follow me. Let's get you situated," Althea says to the arriving group. They grab their bags off the luggage cart in turn and make their way down the tunnel towards the dome.

Hester isn't sure what to make of Althea Ellis. It's hard to get a read on anyone back on Earth with all the mind-numbing substances they take. Althea is probably just a devotee of Hawkins like everyone else Hester met at the

Pentagon, knowing how to prey on the fears of these teens, getting them to trust her.

Hester resolves not to spend too long on this. She's not here to make friends or analyze the captain. She's got a very important job to do, and nothing will get in the way of that.

CHAPTER 6

DREW

"My God, we've landed in a Martian cult," Drew says to Angelo, who laughs nervously. Angelo's Matercopy follows behind them, unable to pick up on Drew's joke. They are the last three to file down the tunnel.

As they near the entrance to the dome, Drew is confused by the sound of birdsong. Their eyes go wide as they step into a huge garden laid out into different sections.

To the right of them is a large, wooden sign marked "Veg Town," with raised beds of tomatoes, lettuces and other edible plants stretching out behind it. Sweeping around in a semi-circle past those are more beds containing blooming flowers and unusual-looking plants. Lights tower over the beds, bathing the whole area in a warm glow.

Althea addresses the group. "Welcome to the gardens! We're very proud of this. They're maintained by the youth here, and we've managed to grow more than enough food to enable us to only need a few items from Earth. Eighty percent of what we eat is grown right here at Constellation."

The garden is peppered with teens working on the various plants. Drew is struck by the colorful jumpsuits they are wearing. Drew can see words and drawings on them, and some even look painted. Each kid has a different-looking suit, which makes Drew wonder if they've personalized them. Clothes that make you stand out are frowned upon back on Earth. Self-expression is saved for inside the home. Drew can't help but feel suspicious as to why it's allowed here.

They look around for the birds they can hear chirping away, but all they can see is the top of the clear dome about fifty feet in the air above them.

Althea spots Drew searching. "Ah, no. The chirping isn't real. We like to have a few soundtracks around the dome and birdsong is a favorite of the residents out here. You may see some tiny robotic bees though, our aerial pollinators that help us grow the plants here."

She focuses on the rest of the new arrivals. "If you're interested in working in the garden, please sign up on your Intralinks once you are given your password and username. There are three rotating teams of sixty kids in all who keep this place fresh and bountiful. It's amazing, right?" She doesn't wait for an answer before continuing, "If you think this is cool, wait 'til you see the forest at the far east end of the dome. We camp out there."

"Camp?" asks Drew, totally confused. "Like, in tents?"

"Yup," replies Althea and then moves on, gesturing for the kids to follow her.

As Drew walks, they notice a tiny floating "bee" whizz by, landing delicately on a nearby plant. It is white and red with silver lattice-shaped wings. Drew watches with fascination as the bee vibrates its wings, shaking out a silvery powder onto the leaves.

They catch up to Angelo and walk through the garden,

finally arriving at a cream-colored building about a quarter of the size of the dome. On one long level with large circular and oval-shaped windows, it looks like an enormous log made out of Swiss cheese.

Althea leads them towards the entrance down the path ahead. Doors open like subway cars, and two more of the AI units in blue uniforms stand on either side.

"These are our 'Bobs'—utility AIs who help with all kinds of things here at Constellation. They do maintenance and perform checks on the dome and outside areas when needed. They can direct you to anywhere you need to go within the dome," says Althea.

"And kick your ass if you step out of line," interrupts a teen boy with dark-colored skin as he steps out of the entrance to the building.

Althea winces a little at this. "Sho. Don't scare them." She turns to the group. "This is Shohiwa. He's from Zimbabwe and grows the best tomatoes on Mars. But yes, these Bobs will keep you on the right path."

Drew shares a look with Angelo. They had two similar AI units in their school. One discovered the drugs in Drew's backpack. Drew had no idea they'd been uploaded with an extremely sensitive olfactory program that allowed them to detect illegal substances.

Drew is pretty sure these "Bobs" are loaded with every surveillance program invented. They resolve to steer clear of them.

Althea walks ahead into the camp building and the kids file in after her. As they go, Ash seems to bump into Sho on purpose. Sho cocks his head slightly, almost curious in expression as he takes Ash in.

"Problem?" says Ash.

"Yah, no," replies Sho, unfazed by Ash's aggression. "We

don't need any alpha bros here at Constellation, my friend. No problem unless you make one."

Ash stares him down. Sho smiles wide, showing a row of brilliant white teeth. Drew can see Ash is trying to figure out how or if to escalate it, but eventually Sho just walks away towards the tomato plants, whistling a song. Ash slouches off into the building.

"Let us follow along, Angelo," says his Matercopy.

"He's such bad news," Angelo says to Drew under his breath. "I feel like he'll kill me in my sleep one night."

"Don't be stupid," Drew replies. "He'll do it in the cafeteria with a poisoned pie at lunchtime."

Angelo punches Drew in the arm.

CHAPTER 7

HESTER

It takes Hester less than thirty minutes to solve sixteen program glitches within the AI operating at Constellation. She takes a break and watches a news conference with President Atlas Hawkins that is being projected from her newly assigned Intralink wristband. She is eating her most recent addiction: a PB&J sandwich on white bread.

Hawkins is speaking about how well the "experiment" on Mars is doing, and his self-congratulatory speech makes Hester want to spit a wad of bread at him. She scowls and closes the screen. Sandwich finished, she stretches out the kinks from the long travel and twelve-hour sleep she enjoyed last night.

The lab at Constellation is large and bright. At one end sit ten long tables, a few of which have AI models on them in various stages of completion or repair. Along the wall, steel cabinets are filled with tools and extra parts.

A round white table has been placed in the middle of the lab, where the staff gather for meetings and communal meals.

At the other end stand three rows of desks and chairs. Ultra-thin curved screens sit on them with flat keyboards below for those who prefer older tech. Hester has five human lab technicians working efficiently around her.

The lab is clean, minimalist and smelling faintly of coffee. Hester is going to enjoy working here. With that thought, the fireflies of tiny pinpoints again dance across her field of vision.

"How are you getting on?"

She blinks and turns to see Althea walking towards her. She is carrying what looks like a male human head with wires protruding from it under her arm.

Thankfully, the lights have gone as quickly as they came, leaving Althea now clear and in focus.

"Great!" Hester replies a little too enthusiastically.

"Wonderful. What are you working on now?"

"I've fixed the irregularities in the older Lehmann models—"

"All of them?"

"Up to version 5.9. That's all I could see listed in my feed? Uh, yeah, so now I'm about to upload worker programs into the new Bobs that were on the ship with us. I wrote some code this morning to make it easier for them to distinguish the ages of the kids and adults in real time."

Althea is a little lost for words. "That's... impressive, Hester. Not a bad first day at work." Then, with a muted thud, she puts the head down onto Hester's desk. "Sorry. It's heavier than it looks," she says with a smirk.

The head looks incredibly life-like, down to the wavy auburn hair, stubble on the face and different pigmentations of color on the skin. The eyes are a gray-blue and Hester can even see faint creases around them. "Lehmann 6.8?"

"Correct." Althea nods. "This is Cadmus, a new therapist. Would love for you to get him up and running."

"Absolutely," replies Hester, trying not to sound too eager.

She is hit by a question and thinks better of it—Hester has a hard time editing herself. But then her curiosity gets the better of her and she blurts, "Your therapist AI units... they are *very* different from the ones I've studied on Earth."

"How so?"

Hester doesn't sense a guarded tone in Althea's voice, so she proceeds. "Their stated objective. Usually they follow a three-step model—ask five questions to determine the personality type of the individual, five questions to prompt the individual to state why they are in therapy and then five to determine how they could improve themselves. And the rest of the sessions are taken up by the patient rattling on in response."

Althea's expression is hard to read. She seems to be sizing up Hester. "It works in certain cases, but I'm not satisfied with that. Not if we want to progress to true healing."

Hester types a few keystrokes on her computer and an image of a figure doing a series of poses appears on her screen. "I'm not crazy, right? That's yoga?"

Althea nods. "It died out in the West after the war but is still practiced in India and other parts of Asia."

"And you have AIs programmed to lead things like meditation, red light therapy, journaling, drawing, as well as their one-on-one sessions?"

"I do. We do," Althea says, gesturing to the others in the lab. "Without my team I couldn't create the programs I think really make a difference."

Hester is torn between being impressed and deeply skeptical. This isn't what she expected from a juvenile prison camp. "Does your boss know? I mean, Commander Whatever-his-name-is..."

"Commander Roberts. No, he doesn't know yet. Is that a problem, Hester?"

Hester shakes her head. "I think anything that could bring them back to life is worth trying."

Althea holds Hester's gaze for a moment, making Hester wish she'd kept her mouth shut, but then she smiles. "Come with me," she says as she grabs the male head.

They walk over to the part of the lab where the AI units are assembled. Amongst the various robotic parts sits a young Asian woman with a shock of dyed white hair cut into a bob. She is staring intently at a transparent screen in front of her that looks like it's floating, suspended from a delicate column hanging from the ceiling. She taps on the screen and then pushes it away from her. It comes to an easy stop in front of the wall of bins.

Althea puts the head down on a nearby table as she addresses the woman. "Wendy? This is Hester. Have you met yet?"

Wendy doesn't look up as she grabs a sleek instrument from the table close by as she says, "Hester. MIT grad. Aced her Machine Learning degree in ten months."

Hester is taken aback.

"Nope. Haven't met yet." Wendy moves her chair over to where another Lehmann model is lying on a table. This one has its head intact. She unceremoniously yanks the head to the right so she can open a small panel at the base of its neck. "Nice to meet you, wunderkind. And this is Damon. He's extremely busy right now too."

"What she lacks in people skills, she makes up for in ability," says Althea.

"That's why you're here, Althea," Wendy retorts. "I'm too busy to manage people's fragile sense of self." She finally looks up and grins. Hester waits for Althea to admonish Wendy, but she just laughs.

Althea's Intralink lights up with a message. She glances at it then turns back to Hester. "Max needs me. Ask me anything, just flag me down or message me on the Intralink," she says, holding up the band. "This reaches me anywhere in the dome."

"OK."

Althea starts to walk away, but then stops. "Oh, can you help Wendy with Damon as well? I need these AIs for sessions this afternoon."

"Sure," replies Hester, excited to finally get her hands on the AIs.

"Great," Althea says and walks out of the lab.

Hester turns back to Wendy, who is now staring intently at her.

"How fast can you program one of these?"

Hester hesitates. She can't decide if she should tell the truth or double the time it really takes her.

"Uh, about an hour," she finally answers.

Wendy purses her lips. "Alright. You've impressed me. I'm impressed," she says grudgingly. Hester is glad she lied. Though now she has to drag it out an extra thirty minutes.

Hester walks over to the incredibly life-like Lehmann AI called Damon. She takes in his inky-brown hair, made of the latest synthetic antimicrobial strands; his round face, which gives him an innocence; the perfectly designed ears. His skin, infused with multiple tones of brown, looks flushed under the lights of the lab. She marvels at the collarbone that has been added to this model and can even see a slight double chin created by the folds of the malleable silicone cover housing his internal parts.

"I'll be finished in five minutes with him and then I'm onto Cadmus," Wendy announces.

Hester nods. As she takes in the shape of Damon's face, the pinpoints of light return and dance across her field of vision. There is an urgency to them she hasn't felt since being here. She quickly turns away from Wendy so she doesn't see, and walks over to where Cadmus's head is. Her whole body starts to hum ferociously as if she's being lit from within.

It's at that moment Hester realizes she has found her guys.

CHAPTER 8

JUNI

As Juni scans the code whizzing across her field of vision, she thinks about seeing Sho again tonight. Her stomach flips in excitement, but she tries to stuff it down. She has to focus on the task at hand, or she'll end up scrambling her visual display and just staring at patterns of static, which Juni does on purpose to fall asleep sometimes.

The implant uses her optical nerve system to absorb the world around her and give real-time data. It also gives her access to sanctioned web pages that are downloaded directly into her brain via the thalamus.

But Juni knows how to get beyond the firewalls and into a much deeper realm of the biochip's capabilities. She discovered dormant wifi code, which she activated and now can connect to Constellation's server.

She frowns and opens her eyes.

I gotta stop doing this.

The punishment for using your biochip on Constellation is severe. It was powered down at her sentencing, but it took five minutes for her to get it working again once she got up here.

Juni is looking for a way into Constellation's mainframe. She can't help it; it's a habit she started in fourth grade. She was amazed at how easy it was to hack into her school's computer. With a thrill she read a few reports of how messed up the kids were, but it quickly became too depressing.

Since then, Juni has hacked into the computers at the museum, the train station, the local football stadium, the utility plant of her city, and the mayor's office (some juicy shit in that one) before proceeding to crypto banks, the US public school main system, and finally the US military base where her father is stationed. That's when she got caught.

By her dad. *The shame.*

And now here she is. Her dad turned her in without a second thought, saying she needed to bear full responsibility for her actions.

The door swings open and Juni quickly taps her biochip to turn it off. A man walks into the small but cozy room and crosses to the chair opposite Juni's. Behind him, Juni can see through the oval window the artificial grow lights shining on the vegetable garden.

The man has auburn hair and blue eyes and smiles warmly at Juni. He wears khaki slacks and a white button-down shirt. As he sits, the third button on his shirt comes undone. He stares at it for a moment before looking at Juni with questioning eyes.

"Wow. You're AI."

"I am. Call me Cadmus. Pleasure to meet you, Juni."

"Very realistic. But still the glitch with buttons?"

Cadmus laughs. "They said it was fixed. Appears untrue." He closes his eyes for a moment, then opens them. "I have reported it to the lab. They will update it in the next version of my model." Then he leans back into his chair. "Now. Tell me about yourself, Juni."

Juni snorts a little. She *hates* therapy. "Why don't *you* tell me about me, Cadmus? I'm sure it's all right there in your database."

Cadmus continues to smile at her as he recites, "Juni Legrosse. Born in West Virginia on January eighth, 2037, to Marshall Legrosse and Pamela Higson. Older sister, Jane, who is twenty-one. Sentenced to eighteen months at Camp Constellation for hacking into the computer system at the NSA Sugar Grove military base." Cadmus pauses. "That's just what happened to you. Not who you are. I'd like to know about *you,* Juni."

If Althea programmed Cadmus, this isn't something she's going to get out of easily. "One question: does Althea download everything I say in these sessions? You're recording all of this, right?"

Cadmus shifts positions. He rests his hands on his knees. "Would you like me to not record?"

Juni raises an eyebrow. "Funny."

"I am allowed to turn off my audio at the request of the patient if it feels prudent."

"Huh." Juni isn't buying it. "And why's that?"

"Because Althea wants trust to be built between us. You can decide to trust me if you wish to. I understand this might take some time."

Juni doesn't know what to say. She's only met Althea twice: once when she first landed three weeks ago, and then during an hour-long intake session, where Althea took a lot of notes even though Juni said barely anything.

"Do you like video games?" asks Cadmus. After a moment, Juni nods. "Why don't we talk about that? I'd like to hear about the ones you've played lately."

"And from that you'll discover everything you need to know about my personality?"

Cadmus laughs. "Just some basic impulses. It will tell me which type you fall into."

"You know what I am already."

"ISTJ. You try to make order out of chaos," answers Cadmus simply.

Juni absorbs this but doesn't respond.

"Would you like to tell me about your life on Earth with your family?"

"I think I'm disowned," she replies casually.

"I doubt that."

"Whatever." She shrugs. "My sister is the smart, good girl who never makes a wrong step, and I'm the sulky girl who has turned to the dark side."

"Do you want to tell me about what it was like growing up?"

For a moment, Juni thinks about leaving. But even if Cadmus reports none of this, it's pretty obvious a three-minute session isn't Juni taking her rehabilitation seriously. The sessions are time-stamped and appear on Juni's schedule throughout her stay at Constellation.

"It was like every other kid's childhood. Super fun 'til you turn five, then you realize you can't go anywhere without being watched. You can only wear black, white and gray. You can't learn about history before the war, you can't push back at anything without being placated, told that you should be grateful there is no crime, there is no need to work 'til twenty-one, you have everything you need, you're totally safe..." She trails off, looking back out at the garden.

"You were trapped," says Cadmus.

She is surprised, laughs a little. "Um... are you allowed to say that?"

"What do you mean? The truth? It sounds to me like a childhood devoid of freedom," replies Cadmus.

"Huh. You're not like my last AI therapist. All she did was ask questions. A lot of frigging questions."

Cadmus just looks at her, his eyes warm and open.

Suddenly, Juni's expression darkens. "What the hell's going on? What kind of bullshit is this?" She jumps out of her chair and looks around the room for a camera.

Cadmus remains seated. "If you would remain calm and explain what you mean, I'm sure I could—"

"You're a goddamn human! What kind of test is this?" she demands, her voice escalating.

"No test, Juni. I am not human. I am a Lehmann Model 6.8, designed in Hamburg and built in New Delhi in February, 2053."

She crosses her arms in front of her. "Prove it."

Cadmus raises his right hand. After a moment, the palm of his hand lights up and Juni can see under the skin a series of numbers illuminated.

"Go on, scan it," says Cadmus.

Juni points the Intralink on her wrist at his palm and says. "Scan."

A floating screen is projected in front of her, and she is shown a series of pictures of robotic parts, wires, silicone moldings of skin at the plant in New Delhi. Then more images of components being placed on the NASA *Intrepid*, and finally a series of Cadmus being assembled in Althea's lab, time-stamped this morning.

The last image is of Cadmus laid out on a table in an all-white jumpsuit and a teen girl with brown curly hair standing next to it. She is wearing a lab coat.

"Who's that?" asks Juni.

"That is Hester. She helped to build me yesterday. I enjoyed meeting her."

"She works in the lab?" Juni remembers what Sho told her in the diner yesterday.

"She does, yes. She told me she is very proud of the fact that she is the youngest military appointee in twenty-five years. So you see, it is OK, Juni. I am what I say I am."

Juni still feels very unnerved. "Yeah, sure. But I'm sorry, I-I just don't feel great. I think I'm getting my period. So I'm gonna go, OK? I'll see you tomorrow…"

She taps her Intralink to close the screen and makes for the door, closing it quickly behind her.

Cadmus sits in the chair staring at the door, his expression placid.

Then he looks down at his button and, with little effort, fastens it.

CHAPTER 9

ATLAS HAWKINS, 85

Atlas Hawkins is losing interest.

He is staring at a clear glass screen protruding from the corner of the *Resolute* desk in the Oval Office. He is waiting for the Indian prime minister to stop talking about the food supply issues in the state of Madhya Pradesh so that he can offer her a new class of mood optimizers just brought to market by his pharmaceutical arm. He picks at a small age spot on his otherwise smooth hands, getting impatient to seal the deal.

"… Respectfully, we had an agreement, Mr. President. My country is still waiting for the remainder of the agriculture tech you promised. We have only received sixty-five percent of what was agreed upon."

"*Respectfully*, you don't have enough *water* to provide your people with the food they need. I am more than willing to ship the tech, Sughanda, but if there ain't no water, it's a waste of time." Atlas chuckles. "Now, we can offer you a deal on the cloud converters that I think you'll be very happy with."

Atlas is tired of dealing with India. Their resistance is messing with his target projections. They have been surprisingly bullish about dealing with the post-war fallout themselves.

The image of Prime Minister Sughanda on the glass freezes. There is a long pause in the room—only a hint of white noise can be heard.

Atlas looks at his new chief of staff, Mary Williams, who is sitting in one of the ten chairs facing the desk. "Did she hang up?"

Mary shakes her head. Then Atlas hears the prime minister clear her throat and her face reappears on screen. "Mr. President. We understand the terms of the contract very clearly. But our construction workers have been forced to work under extreme heat and it is slowing things down."

"Which will be corrected once the machines are making all those pretty puffy clouds that dot the skyline in Delhi, Prime Minister."

"There is also the issue of the change in price..."

Now Atlas sees where this is going. "An unfortunate but necessary decision, but if it makes you feel any better, the UK, Canada and Russia are all paying more. And let's not forget you and China are the first in line for any emerging tech, a full six months' head start. Now *that's* a great deal, wouldn't you say?"

Another frozen image. Atlas rolls his eyes.

"I understand, Mr. President," says Prime Minister Sughanda eventually in a measured tone. "I would also like to ask when we can receive a report on how the camp is doing on Mars. We have twenty-three citizens there, as you know..."

Atlas doesn't know. And he doesn't care. "My chief of staff tells me things are going as planned. We have the first offenders returning to Earth in three days on NASA *Intrepid*, hopefully cured of all those criminal tendencies." He chuckles.

"Okay, thank you. We shall speak soon, yes? I wish you and your family—"

Atlas presses a button, ending the call. The glass screen disappears into the desk. It has been coated in a glossy white paint, flecked with reflective silver particles. On a sunny day, Atlas can see his reflection in it.

He addresses Mary. "Call her chief of staff and tell them there was a glitch on the line. And get them to agree to purchasing the new drugs."

She nods.

Atlas spins his chair around and looks out of the floor-to-ceiling windows onto the tennis court and pool area. He demolished the old White House when he became president during the war and built a new one with 3D-printed construction. Designed by AI programs, it now towers over Pennsylvania Avenue, looking more like an ultra-modern hotel than the seat of government.

"I'm tired of the ingratitude, Mary," Atlas sighs.

"I understand, sir," she commiserates.

"The fate of the world was hanging in the balance after GabDC12. Some countries disappeared altogether. Did you know that?"

"I did... *not*, sir," Mary answers carefully.

"Oh, yes. And if it wasn't for my air-cleansing tech, the rest of us would be living underground by now. And yet here we are twenty years on from the war with virtually no crime, no unrest, no racism, no sexism, no economic misery..."

Mary hesitates. Atlas glares at her.

"It's a fantastic time to be alive, Mr. President," she finally says.

Atlas nods. "And all because of what I achieved." He points to a digital map of Earth on the wall to the right of him. "We now have the Americas, Europe, Russia, most of Asia and what is left of Oceania under our wing," he boasts as he looks at the countries with an American flag in the middle of them.

China and India have no such flag. He can almost hear them taunting him from the map. He fights the urge to smash it.

"I want them, Mary. I want their weapons tech, and I want compliance," he growls.

Atlas reaches into his jacket and pulls out a small flask. He takes a swallow of his longevity serum, coded only for his DNA, and relaxes his shoulders.

"Mr. President, I will get these optimizers circulating in their population one way or the other."

This is what he wants to hear. He knew he made the right decision in hiring her. She's young and ambitious, and who knows? Should he need an heir apparent (or fall guy), she could be perfect.

"That will be all, Mary."

Mary nods and leaves the room.

Atlas turns to his AI unit, Oliver, who is standing at the far end of the room. He has no hair and looks less human than the other Lehmann 6.8 models, at Atlas's request. He wants the processing power of a 6.8, but Atlas likes his AI to look like what they really are—*tools*.

"Do we have the latest plans drawn up for Constellation City?"

"We do," says Oliver, his voice thin and devoid of any inflection.

"Show me."

Oliver projects a large floating screen in front of Atlas. A dome-shaped structure becomes visible in the middle of the screen with the words "Camp Constellation, completed 2053" floating above it. Then the image morphs as another 3D structure is imposed on top of it. As it settles over the camp, it begins to expand out into a series of buildings.

"Constellation City, 2058" is now visible above.

"Bigger," says Atlas, smiling.

They expand further.

"Bigger," he demands again, until the plans for a city reach almost to the walls of the Oval Office. There are signs for hotels, a shopping mall, a spa and even a doggy daycare.

Atlas leans back in his chair, grinning.

Now that is a thing of beauty.

CHAPTER 10

HESTER

Hester is slowly finding her way around Constellation. She's impressed with the fact that it feels more like a school campus than a penal colony. So far, she's located the diner (odd, but cute), the gym (which she'll never use), and the charging area for the Lehmann AIs. She met Glykeria in there, a Lehmann model who is used for the meditation circles and red light therapy sessions that are supposed to help heal trauma in the body. Glykeria offered to give her a lesson in meditation, but Hester politely declined.

She's done a good job of avoiding interactions with the other teens and intends to keep it that way, though she has to admit to herself that she has felt lonely at times. She almost offered to buy Drew a Starburst latte earlier when they were in line at the diner but shook the impulse off.

As she makes her way down the corridor of the east wing of the building, her attention is caught when she passes by an open door. The unmistakable white hair of Wendy is half-covering a 3D image of a human brain on the screen in front of her, rotating slowly. Hester moves in closer and can see the words "Althea Ellis" above the brain.

Wendy turns at the sound of Hester entering the room.

"Hey, Wendy. What's up?" Hester walks inside. The room looks like a doctor's office—low lighting, neutral walls. In front of her is a reclining gray chair. A sleek black circle is resting on it.

"What's this?" Hester picks up the halo. She can see digital lights on the side.

Wendy gets up and slaps Hester lightly on the hand, taking the halo out of her grasp. "Careful! This is highly sensitive equipment."

"Sorry," says Hester, admonished.

Wendy gently places the halo back on the chair. "It's our memory capture and retrieval program. We call it TIM. We're beta-testing it now."

Interest piqued, Hester moves closer to the screen. "Cool. So you mean like taking someone's memories for playback?"

Wendy nods. "The aim is to download it in such detail, the patient can go next door and be fully immersed in their memories."

"Nice… and this is Althea's?"

"Yeah. We map the brain in its entirety first and then start the download phase. She'll be the first to test it."

Hester is mesmerized by the different patterns of Althea's brain. She finds the grooves and curves endlessly fascinating. They remind her of the patterns made by waves pushing into the sand as they lap in the same spot over and over. As the brain rotates, Hester pictures mountains and valleys where the areas become denser—a whole ecosystem packed into such small real estate. It really is such a beautiful design. Inefficient, but beautiful.

Wendy's Intralink beeps. She pats her pockets. A flicker of

panic crosses her eyes. "Uh, gotta go. I left something back at the lab." She gets up and crosses to the door. "Don't touch anything!" she calls over her shoulder as she pulls the door closed behind her and heads down the corridor.

But Hester doesn't follow orders well. Curious, she taps on the desk and a flat keyboard appears lit up. The program is like child's play for her and, within a few seconds, she closes out Althea's file and opens a new one.

She grabs the halo from the chair and rests it on her head. *This should be fun.*

Hester starts the mapping sequence and can feel the halo vibrating. It's quite pleasant.

Starting as small as a walnut, the image in front of Hester begins to emerge. At first, the left half of the brain starts to be written in code, mapped perfectly as a replica on the screen. But as the right side starts to take shape, the program slows down.

Hester's eyes widen as the program attempts to map the right side of her brain.

In that moment, she hears something behind her. She quickly hits "delete" on the keyboard and pulls the halo off her head. Turning to put the halo back on the chair, she sees the door is slightly ajar. Althea is standing there.

"Oh, hi!" Hester blurts. "Uh, this is fascinating. Wendy told me about it. Memory capture and retrieval…" Hester can feel a surge of energy inside her and tries to calm herself, worried the pinpoints might decide to make an appearance.

Althea pushes the door open a little. She blinks a few times before answering, "Yes. We're hoping it can be used to process trauma in a healthy way. If all goes to plan, that is…"

There is an awkward moment as Althea seems on the edge of saying more. But she just smiles politely and steps into the room. She walks to the chair and picks up the halo. She holds it up in the light, turning it over in her hands. Hester realizes she is examining it.

"Okay, great. Well, good luck with it," blusters Hester as she salutes Althea and walks out. She immediately regrets the salute.

As Hester makes her way back to the lab, she resolves to be more cautious.

Cadmus, assigned qualities of a 25-year-old male

Cadmus is walking Angelo to the door of his office. It is the last session of the day. "Goodbye, Angelo," he says.

Angelo nods and walks away, stuffing his hands into his pockets. Cadmus then steps out into the hallway and closes his office door.

Cadmus watches Angelo for a moment as he uploads his session notes into the camp's data cloud. Cadmus notes that his processor is absorbing more language models as he speaks to the humans in his care. Today, he has learned from his patients the slang "uptiming" and "downtiming" (working and relaxing), "chars" (one's close friends), and "kerned," which refers to an awkward moment or situation.

As he processes the session with Angelo, he replays the way Angelo did not want to talk, his body language and lack of eye contact. Cadmus deduces from his session that the boy is potentially depressed. As he notes that perhaps Angelo would be more comfortable with his Matercopy present, he sees a code he does not recognize. He scans his entire processor but can only find it in his therapy program.

He closes his eyes and reports it to the lab.

As he turns to walk down the corridor, he sees a male AI

unit coming towards him, side-stepping to allow Angelo to pass by freely.

Cadmus registers the appearance of this other unit—the hair cut close to the head, the dark skin, the white button-down shirt and khaki pants.

The unit smiles at Cadmus as he gets closer.

"Hello. I am Damon," says the AI to Cadmus.

"Hello. I am Cadmus."

The unit called Damon lifts his right palm, and Cadmus immediately downloads Damon's historical blueprint. Then Cadmus does the same for Damon to download.

"You are a Lehmann," says Damon.

"Yes."

Damon passes Cadmus, continuing his path.

He is a few feet away when Cadmus finds himself saying, "Do you ever wonder what it is like to be a child?"

Damon stops walking. He turns to face Cadmus. "I do not."

They stare at each other.

"But I do wonder what it is like to be you."

CHAPTER 11

SHO, 17

Sho is freshly showered. He brushes his teeth, puts on the gold ring his father gave him on his sixteenth birthday, and takes stock of himself in the mirror.

"Look at you just now. Not bad, Shohiwa." He laughs at himself.

It's been a long time since Sho smiled easily. Since he was happy. For a long time Sho thought that "happy" had been squeezed out of his soul for good. That it was gone from his whole family. He misses them deeply. He was sad back in Bulawayo, knowing life could be so much better, but he still loves his home.

Sho was allowed to work in his father's restaurant because he was so tall he passed for twenty-one. No one bothered to check his credentials because everybody in Bulawayo knew and loved the food his father cooked. Recipes handed down by his grandmother and aunt made people feel as close to happy as they could, being so zoned out from all the drugs they took to "manage."

Now he closes his eyes and can almost smell the delicious Dovi stew boiling on the back burner of the ancient stove in the kitchen there. He can see his father sharing stories with the locals, talking over a beer about the latest gossip in town, or commiserating over the lack of sports to watch.

Sho's father is a good man. He helps people whenever he can. And that is why Sho couldn't bear to see him threatened. No one had the right to take his father's livelihood from him. Or his dignity.

Sho's Intralink beeps. It is six-ten p.m.

He opens the bathroom door that leads back into the dormitory that he shares with eighteen other boys.

Seated on one of the beds is the new kid Angelo's Matercopy. Her hands are folded in her lap and her eyes are closed. On the bedside table at the end of the bed, Sho can see a small white box with a rectangular battery pack about the size of a deck of cards. A digital display on the box reads "62% charged…"

Sho sits on his bed a few feet away and puts on his shoes. As he looks up, the Korean kid Ash is now kneeling on Angelo's bed behind the Matercopy. He reaches over her and puts his hand on the left side of her chest. He calls out to another boy, who turns and laughs as Ash begins to squeeze her silicone breast.

Sho jumps up. "Hey! What's wrong with you?"

Ash turns at the sound and stands up. He is a few inches smaller, but he is as well-built as Sho is.

"What's wrong with *you?* It's a stupid doll. What, you got one of these at home? Do you sleep with it at night?" says Ash, his words stilted but the taunt knife-sharp. He laughs in Sho's face.

Chill, Sho, he's not worth it.

But then Ash has to go and grab for Sho's chest. Sho gives

him a quick, hard shove and Ash now faces the ceiling, his body flat out on the ground.

Sho instantly regrets it. Not because he feels guilty, but because he's afraid he won't get to see Juni tonight. And this thought makes him even angrier.

Not one to quit easily, Ash manages to get on his knees and tackles Sho around his waist. Sho falls backwards onto his bed. Ash gets one punch to Sho's ribcage before two Bobs burst in the door, alerted by the unusual pattern of sounds coming from inside.

One of the Bobs grabs Ash effortlessly off Sho. "Stop, Ash Deung," she demands as her facial recognition kicks in.

Ash refuses. He starts to struggle and pull away, but the Bob has him firmly in her grip. She then looks at Sho, who knows it's a lost battle. "Shohiwa Moyo. You are coming with me."

The other Bob stands behind Sho and Ash as they walk out of the dorm to face the consequences of their foolishness.

Sho just hopes Juni will forgive him for standing her up.

Juni

"Love is bullshit."

"You swear a lot, do you know that?"

Juni scowls at Drew. They sip banana milkshakes as they listen to the sound of a windpipe drowning in its own mellowness, echoing through the speakers in the diner.

"God, this music really is grim. So, the guy you're talking about is Sho? I met him yesterday in the garden," says Drew after another gulp.

Juni nods. She can't believe Drew already knows she's into

Sho, and that he has stood her up. But there's something about Drew that she instantly liked. She sat next to them in drawing class this afternoon and their picture of a kitten trying to eat the tail of a massive dragon made her laugh.

"He seems cool, actually," says Drew.

"Then you date him," retorts Juni. Drew chuckles.

"I get it now. Why they don't allow us to date on Earth 'til twenty-one. 'Cause they don't want us all moaning constantly about some idiot who can't tell time. For example."

She's tempted to try and hack into the Intralink network and find out where Sho is, but decides he isn't worth the effort.

Drew smiles and finishes their milkshake.

"You ever had a crush on anyone?" Juni asks.

Drew is silent for a moment then shrugs. "It's pointless, right?"

Juni isn't convinced they mean that, but doesn't push it.

"So—is it just me or is Althea maybe not a complete dictator? I had my intake interview with her this morning and I dunno, she didn't seem all that bad," Drew says as they fiddle with their new Intralink band.

"She's not the worst adult I've been around, I guess."

"It's just—I expected this place to be really bleak, and it's not. It's unsettling, to be honest. And there was a girl getting on the ship the other day who literally didn't want to go back. Crying like a baby. All the kids leaving were hugging Althea like she was their mother or something. Freaked me out."

Juni's not surprised. Even in the few short weeks she's been here, she has felt... *different.* She hasn't wanted to admit it to herself, but she has started to feel more relaxed. Something about this place makes her feel like she is safer than on Earth. And it's frigging Mars. Middle of nowhere. It scares her and yet she doesn't want to be afraid anymore either. "I don't know what their endgame is here, dude, but I'll reserve judgment 'til my time is up."

"How long do you have?"

"Eighteen months and three weeks. You?"

"Two years."

"Wow. What did you do?"

Drew hesitates. Juni suddenly feels like she might have overstepped. "Sorry. I'm too nosy for my own good."

Drew looks out the window. Juni just wants to go to her dorm and hack. Forming friendships is a waste of goddamn time here. And she sucks at it.

She's about to tell Drew that she needs to go when they say, "I got caught selling drugs with my cousin Angelo at school."

"Whoa!" replies Juni, wide-eyed. "How did you get them? Man, I wish I went to your school."

Drew laughs. "You'd hate it. It's no better in England, Juni. We're treated like infants there too."

"Yeah, but at least I'd be high so I wouldn't care," she replies. "I would give anything to forget this monotonous life for a while."

Drew nods. "My parents own a chemist's."

Juni frowns.

"A pharmacy," Drew clarifies. "They got a Hawkins franchise five years ago. It was a really big deal. That license to sell his drugs made them the busiest in Finchley."

Now Juni gets it. "And so you stole the drugs from there?"

"Yeah. My dad had a few other compounds in the back. I started reading up on what they were on the pre-web and Bob's your uncle, I found a combo that made me think I was really talking to those kittens and dragons in the local high street."

Juni is impressed but confused. "A 'Bob' is your uncle?"

Drew's face lights up. "It's a British saying. It means 'and just like that,'" they say through their laughter.

Juni likes that she made them laugh. She relaxes a little, thinking she might have found a new friend after all.

As she sips on her milkshake, Juni becomes aware that a boy is standing a few feet away from them. His hair is messy and his white jumpsuit has been buttoned up incorrectly. He's holding a tray with a limp Galactic Burrito on it. She has no idea how long he's been there.

She smiles, but he doesn't smile back right away, like he's deciding something.

"Hey," she says brightly, trying to break the ice.

At this, Drew looks up and turns. "Oh, hey, Angelo."

Juni isn't sure what to do, as it's a two-person booth. The indecision is enough for Angelo to start to walk away.

"Do you want to pull up a chair? This is Juni," says Drew finally. They look around for a spare chair, but there aren't any in close range.

Angelo shakes his head. "Nah, you're OK." He finds a table close by and sits down by himself.

"Do you want to go over there? It's totally fine if you do," Juni says.

Drew stares at Angelo, who keeps his head down as he starts to eat.

"I'm good," they finally answer.

"That's your cousin, right?"

"Yeah, but doesn't mean we need to act like we're married, does it?"

"O-kaaay."

"Sorry. I just... need some space, that's all. Angelo's cool. It's just..." Drew trails off, unable to finish.

Juni decides not to push it. She's uncomfortable with

Drew's discomfort. *Who needs more of that?* "Hey, all good. Tell me more about these angry kitten drugs."

Drew laughs.

CHAPTER 12

SHO

Sho is shown into a large room by the female Bob. Behind him, Ash is walked in by the other one. There is a row of chairs along one wall and most of the floor is taken up by soft rubber mats.

"Wait here," orders the female Bob. She leaves her male counterpart with them and exits.

Ash walks over to one of the chairs and slumps down in it. Sho remains standing, adrenaline still coursing through his body. He looks at posters on the walls of figures in different yoga poses. In amongst them, he can also see posters of people engaged in what looks like martial arts.

Sho caught a movie once on the pre-web called *Kung Fu Hustle*. He'd never seen anything like it before. All movies with violence in them were banned before Sho was even born. But they were still out there for any enterprising teens with the will to find them.

Through the door walks a man with dark hair wearing a

white shirt with khaki pants. He nods to the male Bob, who turns and leaves.

It takes Sho a minute to register that this is, in fact, an AI unit. He is unnerved by how incredibly life-like he appears—much more defined than Angelo's Matercopy.

"Hello," says the AI unit, "I am Damon."

Ash just shrugs, but Sho responds, "Hey. I'm Sho."

"Pleasure to meet you, Sho," says Damon. He looks at Ash. "And also you, Ash Deung."

"When do we get to leave?" replies Ash, sounding bored.

"That depends," Damon says as he walks over to a small round cushion on one of the mats and sits down.

"On what?" answers Sho.

"On whether you'd like to learn a new way to communicate."

"Huh?" says Ash, irritated.

"If you wish to learn jiujitsu, I will show you some moves, and you can leave after that. If you do not wish to stay, you may go now and I will report this to Althea. I cannot say what will happen after that."

Sho is intrigued. This is a new class of AI he hasn't seen before. "I'm interested."

"Oh, I am pleased." Damon stands and crosses to Sho. He bows to him. "Now you."

Ash snorts, but Sho ignores him. He bows back to Damon, who says, "Jiujitsu is over five hundred years old. Its guiding principle is to yield to your opponent's force"—Ash laughs sarcastically. Damon looks at him placidly—"and then redirect that force back towards your opponent."

Sho is confused. Damon notices. "It is a fluid discipline, asking of the participant a willingness to be like water. One must be prepared to act decisively and change a plan quickly to win a battle. May I show you?"

Sho nods.

"I want you to punch me," Damon states. Sho hesitates.

"It is OK. Remember, I shall not bleed," Damon adds with an awkward chuckle. "Go ahead. And don't hold back. Your objective is to land a punch in my face. No matter what I do, act like I am your worst enemy and make sure you get that punch in."

Sho catches Ash's expression from the sidelines—he now looks *very* interested.

Praying this isn't some weird way to get himself in further trouble, Sho steps forward and throws a pretty mean punch at Damon, expecting him to back up and try to dodge it. To his surprise, Damon actually lunges forward into him as he throws the punch, dodging it and grasping him around the chest.

Sho falters for a moment.

"Keep trying!" says Damon. Sho can't get enough power in his arm to land a punch at the AI's face. He's being hugged too tightly by Damon, who has his face buried in Sho's chest.

Then Damon says, "Enough."

They break apart. Sho is a little out of breath but enjoys the rush of adrenaline through his body.

"This is an important lesson in jiujitsu. You find the weakness in your opponent's move and focus on that as the way to disarm them. Always be looking for the vulnerability."

Damon bows to Sho again and Sho bows back. They step back from each other and then Damon turns. "Ash, I would like you to step forward."

Rolling his eyes, Ash steps onto the mat and, before Damon has a chance to speak, Ash tries to grab him around the waist to take him down. Damon plants his feet firmly on the mat hip-width apart. Even though Ash is pushing as hard as he can, Damon is like a thick tree—totally immovable.

Finally, Ash gives up. "You are AI. Not a fair fight."

"Try me, then," interjects Sho, trying not to laugh at Ash's failed attempt. Ash wheels around to face Sho, his nostrils flaring in anger.

Damon holds up his hand. "Not yet," he says to them both. "You must first learn how to warm up. How to breathe properly and get your bodies prepared to engage."

The two boys size each other up. Sho is just waiting for Ash to jump at him. He can sense the rage ready to leap out of him. Sho has known boys like this before—tormented inside and blaming everyone else for it.

Deciding to rise above it, Sho breaks eye contact with Ash and looks at Damon. "I would like to learn more."

"Oh, I am pleased," says Damon. He looks at Ash expectantly. "Do you wish to continue? If not, you are welcome to leave now."

Ash does nothing for a moment. Then he sulks over to the chairs and sits.

"Okay then. We shall begin again," says Damon.

Sho tries not to get too excited at the thought of some day knocking Ash on his ass.

CHAPTER 13

DREW

Drew and Angelo are sitting in one of the comms pods outside the main building. If the weather is good, the kids can reach home for ten minutes each and talk to their families.

Drew has a very tearful mother on the link. The screen is a little pixelated, but they can see her well enough. She says their father is still at work, which Drew is skeptical of given the time of day back home, but doesn't feel like pushing it. They wouldn't really know what to say to him anyway.

"Are you eating? Hi, Angelo, are you OK?" she says, after seeing Angelo behind Drew midway through her sentence.

"Hi, Aunt Nihira," replies Angelo. "I'm alright."

Drew isn't so sure. Angelo didn't eat yesterday or today. He got mad at his Matercopy this morning in the cafeteria. She mentioned that he wasn't eating enough nutrients to stay in optimal health. He swore at her and stormed out of the cafeteria. Drew held the Matercopy back and made her wait a minute before following Angelo—it always works for Drew. They probably should have gone themselves, but Angelo makes them feel so irritable right now. They know it's irrational but can't help it.

"He's alright, Mum. Are you alright?" Drew asks, burying their anxiety over their cousin.

They instantly regret this. She starts crying again. "Oh, Drew. It's all our fault. If we had just been more vigilant… We never thought about that back room—"

"Mum, Mum. It's not your fault, okay? It's on me."

"But you're not supposed to have these desires, Drew. Your father and I must have missed a step somewhere in the parenting algorithm. I keep looking it over but I can't see it," she chokes through her tears.

She grabs at something off screen and swallows two pills with a glass of water.

At the sight of this, Drew feels as if gravity is pushing hard on them. Guilt is thick in their throat. They glance at Angelo, who is just staring at the floor.

"Mum, listen to me. You followed the rules, OK? I-I can't explain it, but I just wanted to try it. Now I see I was wrong."

"You tried it? Oh, God, Drew! I thought you were just giving it to other students!" she wails.

Angelo whispers to Drew, "Mate, seriously? You tried it without me?"

Drew signals for Angelo to shut up. He snorts in response and turns his back on Drew. They roll their eyes. "I'm sorry, Mum. They're helping me here, OK? I'm working on making sure I don't slip up again."

Drew's mother doesn't answer right away. She slows her breathing and closes her eyes, the blanket of chemicals now wrapping themselves around her.

Drew's shoulders slump—they've seen this transition more times than they can count.

"I understand, Drew. Just do your best, please. I know you can do it." Her tone is thick and heavy now.

They see the washed-out look in their mother's eyes and her placid smile and they can't take it anymore.

"Time's up, Mum," says Drew softly. They wave and close the link.

They suddenly feel so tired they want to sleep for a week.

CHAPTER 14

ALTHEA

"Are you sure about this?"

Althea can see the concern on Max's face as he finishes downloading the memory she has chosen into the TIM program. She is sitting in the office with the reclining chair, black halo on her head.

"I'm sure. It needs to be something intense, Max. I want to make sure the detail is as rich as it can be."

On the screen they can see TIM absorbing the neuronic pattern created by Althea's brain as she recalled the event from her past.

"Download complete," comes the soft, low voice of TIM.

Althea takes off the halo and gets off the chair. "Okay, let's see if this was worth all the groveling I had to do with Roberts."

She opens the door and steps into the corridor. The nearest door to her looks different from the others. It is made of thick, soundproof steel and has a "No Entry" sign on it. A blue light is flashing above the keypad.

Althea takes a breath and places her palm on the pad. The light turns green and she steps inside, closing the door behind her.

"Welcome, Althea Ellis," says TIM.

The walls are a pale blue. Althea walks over to one and runs her hand over the padded texture of it. The beige floor is soft underfoot, and the soundproofing in the room makes it so that her movements are muted.

It would be a nice room to nap in if it weren't for the fact she's about to jump back in time.

"Memory retrieval playback starting in three, two, one..."

A panel opens in the ceiling above her head, and millions of tiny beads descend. They hang in the air for a split second like a swarm of locusts deciding which way to escape, but then ultrasonic waves fill the room and morph them into various shapes.

Althea is amazed to watch them being transformed into a fully rendered hologram. Within moments, she is engulfed in a living, breathing rendition of her memory that she can see and touch everywhere around her.

She's taken back to September twenty-fifth, 2052.

Althea finds herself stuck with a procession of other people trailing President Hawkins around his newest pharmaceutical plant. She is amazed by how real it feels inside the memory. She can even smell the hint of fumes emanating from the machine room as she walks.

"We built this place in less than two months using my

patented 3D-printing technology," the president announces to murmurs of admiration from the crowd. To Althea, the building from the outside looks like a frozen wave—about to crush the people inside it at any moment.

As the president drones on about the latest advancements in his mood optimizers, Althea remembers she needs to take hers. As she pats her pockets, she has the sinking feeling she forgot to pack them. The agitation she is starting to feel is not only because she keeps being ignored by Hawkins.

Her superior, Commander Roberts, is standing in line next to her. He is clocking her searching and it makes her even more stressed.

Desperate to wrap things up, she says, "Sir, is this going to go on much longer?"

"Keep your voice down," Roberts demands and pulls her out of the line away from the others.

Althea is startled at the sensation of his arm on hers. The ground under her feet is solid and unyielding and she can feel the flow of the air purifiers blowing down her neck.

Once they are out of earshot Roberts lets go of her arm. "We need a little more gratitude from you, Captain Ellis. It's an honor to be selected to oversee the Constellation program. Yes, the compensation is less than what you were making at the VA, but that's more than made up for by the prestige of being a part of something historic."

"I am extremely grateful, sir, and I am up to the task, but I only want to know if he'll sign off on some new upgrades to the AI programs. It's been three months and I can't get an answer! I think there's a real chance here to help these kids—"

"*Help* them?" replies Roberts. "Ellis, these are criminals. Your job is make sure they don't kill each other up there."

Althea is starting to feel like she is being squeezed from all sides. She must catch herself, as this is too important to mess up. It takes all her willpower to regulate her breathing. "I-I understand, sir. I promise you and the president can count on me," she says as evenly as possible.

"Good," replies Roberts as he looks over in Hawkins's direction.

The president is now being handed a stack of hats with the inscription "The Future is Atlas" by his AI Lehmann model. He throws them out to the visitors, who are forced to grab for them.

Then Hawkins looks over at Althea and Roberts. He shakes his head *no*, then turns back to the crowd. "We're on target to supply two thirds of the world's adult population with our latest class of mood optimizers by January," he boasts. The crowd applauds.

"No upgrades. No deviations. Is that clear?" Roberts says to Althea.

"Yes, sir," Althea replies, burning inside. Her vision is blurring, her throat constricts, and she desperately needs water.

In that moment, Althea-of-the-present has the bizarre sensation of *wanting* to experience the panic attack that is about to happen.

Althea is at once curious and terrified at the thought of withdrawal from her meds. She's seen enough patients who bear the scars of the war and cannot function without them. Their nightmares, their sorrows, their failures—all gone within a few minutes of taking a Hawkins pill. The horror of the past swallowed up by chemistry.

But Althea can't stop thinking about what it would be like to live free of them.

As she lifts up her shaking palms, she remembers this was the moment in her memory when, recognizing her state, Roberts pulled her out of the room and found her some meds. Not out of care, but out of not wanting to be embarrassed in front of the president by his foolish appointee.

"Captain?" says Roberts.

The dawning realization on his face is evident as he witnesses what is happening to her. He goes to grab for her, but she yells, "No!"

She pulls away from him and is amazed that the memory is now no longer as it was—TIM is creating a new version where she can do and say whatever she chooses.

She backs away from him.

It's working!

"Captain Ellis. Do not test me."

"Go to hell," she finds herself saying. She is shocked by the intensity in her voice. Roberts blinks as he registers the insult, then his face hardens.

"Get a hold of yourself! You are about to jeopardize the whole program. Come with me right now and fix this," Roberts hisses.

Althea wants to scream at him. She can feel rage swelling inside of her, pushing the anxiety up and out of the way.

Does she let it overtake her completely?

Even in this memory playback, Althea is afraid of letting it all go.

She is suddenly plunged into blackness. Without a single crack of light around her, she loses her bearings.

"TIM? What's going on?" she shouts, her voice shaking a little.

As her words echo through the dark, she begins to feel a searing heat at her back. The force of it almost pushes her over.

The darkness surrounding her is now streaked with red and orange as she realizes she can smell fire.

Althea spins and is shocked to find herself looking at a

teen girl with long dark hair and piercing blue eyes. The girl is kneeling down on the ground while flames are surging all around her.

Althea starts to fight for breath as the oxygen is being swallowed up by the fire, cracking and popping as it rises higher. She watches in awe as the girl calmly stands up and stares right at her. Her lack of fear stuns Althea as she begins to walk forward.

As she gets closer, Althea is mesmerized by the skin on her face and arms. It's glowing brightly, as if the fire is inside of her.

The girl is inches away now. She leans forward and Althea freezes in place.

"Get mad, Althea. It's time," she says, her breath icy cool on Althea's face.

Suddenly, her skin ripples with goosebumps as she remembers this was a dream. *Her* dream. One she had the first night she arrived on Mars.

"Althea? The program froze…"

In an instant, the girl and the flames are gone when a bright light streaks through the room as Max opens the door behind Althea.

"Whoa, are you OK?" He looks concerned as he takes in Althea's expression.

She cannot answer right away. She tries to catch her breath as the haze of needing her meds begins to seep away. She blinks as her eyes adjust to the light from the corridor outside and she is brought back to the reality of being at Camp Constellation.

"I-I'm OK, Max," she finally replies. "But TIM accessed my subconscious during the download phase and pulled out a dream. One I didn't remember having at the time, but now I sure as hell do."

"That's not good." Max's brow furrows. "Wait—you've been *dreaming?*"

She shakes her head. "Only once. The night we arrived here on Mars."

She walks past him into the office next door. Max follows and they cross to the desk.

"What did TIM log before the program froze?" Althea asks.

"Uh… heart rate, spatial coordinates, neuronic pattern mapping—"

"No dialogue?"

"Not that I can see. But I can override it and retrieve audio…"

Althea scans the screen looking for any anomalies, but programming isn't her specialty. "We need to find the glitch before the kids start using it. Memories only. Otherwise, we can't work with it," she says, wiping a bead of sweat off her forehead.

"Althea, I think this is a mistake."

"Max—"

"No, look at you! You look upset. Like, *really* unnerved."

She grabs Max by the shoulders, staring intently at him. "You're right. It feels amazing."

CHAPTER 15

SHO

Sho is late for his electrical engineering class. His body aches from learning jiujitsu yesterday with Damon. Ash had slouched around the room for most of the night, eventually performing two triangle sit-ups and a shrimp before getting angry and slumping back down in a chair. But Sho appreciated getting to distill the wild bursts of energy he regularly feels into calculated moves.

Mornings are for lessons on Constellation. The afternoons are taken up with various kinds of therapies. Therapy isn't popular where Sho lives. From what he can gather, most kids here have never heard of therapy for under twenty-ones.

He tries to hide his large frame as he enters the room, hoping he'll be ignored. The AI teacher, Electra, is discussing the propeller motion for making drones.

"Thank you for joining us, Shohiwa," Electra says. Her voice shows no trace of sarcasm, which is all the more irritating when Sho's Intralink flashes the words, *5 camp credits deducted for being 3 minutes, 45 seconds late.*

No milkshake for him tonight.

Sho crosses to a table where the kid called Drew is working. He sits next to them and nods a greeting.

"Now, please tap your Intralink for the instructions. You have fifteen minutes on the timer starting now," Electra continues.

Everyone taps their Intralink bands. All around the room 3D holographic instructions for the drones appear in different languages projected in front of them. Sho stares at the parts laid out in front of him and within a few seconds he can see two pieces that should fit together. With a satisfying *click* of circuit onto the board, he is away.

As he finds his flow putting together the propeller pieces and attaching it to the main body, he can feel a pair of eyes staring at him. He looks up.

"Impressive. A hobby at home?" asks Drew.

"No. I cook back at home," Sho responds simply. He picks up the small screwdriver and begins to wire the propeller to the main body of the drone.

"What about in school?" Drew says. Sho shakes his head. As the other kids continue to work on their propellers, Sho puts the last piece in place and turns it on. The propeller unfolds like the petals on a flower and it rises in the air.

His classmates look up with a mixture of envy and admiration as the little drone whizzes over their heads.

"Uh... I think you're meant for more than cooking, mate," says Drew with a smirk. "Any chance you wanna do mine?"

Sho glances sideways at Drew. "Cooking is life, my friend."

Drew's face falls, but then Sho grins and Drew relaxes a little.

But it makes Sho think—maybe there is more to life than

what is waiting for him when he gets out of here. His intelligence has always been underestimated because of his imposing size. Only his parents really understood that his brain is like a primed canvas, ready for vibrant colors.

CHAPTER 16

JUNI

Juni bites her lip as she waits for the door to open. She is standing in the west corridor where the therapy offices are. She has a sinking feeling she's been caught snooping around Constellation's server.

Max opens the door and invites her into the dimly lit room. There are neutral colors on the wall, and a painting of waves crashing on a beach is hung opposite her. Juni recognizes it as student art from a recent class assignment—it's not *totally* terrible.

Althea is perched on a desk in the room, which has a large floating screen above it. "Thanks for coming, Juni," she says.

Max closes the door behind her and she prepares for the worst. "Am I in trouble?" she says with an innocent expression, though her insides are churning.

"No."

Juni looks at Max, but he gives nothing away. "Then why am I here?" she asks, still not ready to let her guard down.

"I just need to make it very clear that this conversation is confidential," interjects Max. He throws a look to Althea, who gives him a small nod in return.

"Thank you, Max." She turns back to Juni. "Your immense skill as a coder needs redirection. Your Comp Sci teacher reported not only that you complete your assignments easily, but that she gave you a challenge to create a curriculum for the whole class for the coming weeks, and she couldn't find any flaws."

Althea types a few strokes on the flat keyboard set into the desk. An image of a human brain appears on the screen. It rotates slowly. Althea places her finger on the screen where the brain is hovering and slows it to a stop, revealing a side view. She touches the base of the brain, and a large bubble appears with the words "Primary Visual Cortex."

"All visual stimuli enter the brain from the eyes into the PVC here," Althea says. She then touches two other parts of the brain, and the words "Hippocampus" and "Prefrontal Cortex" appear. "And these areas are where our memories are stored." She turns to Juni. "Have you heard of memory capture and retrieval?"

Juni's first instinct is to bolt. She has, but doesn't think she should say it was when she was hacking into the military base computer.

Althea smiles. "It's okay, Juni. You're already here serving your sentence. It's not like I don't know what you did."

Juni relaxes her stance a little—she has a point. "Yeah. I saw emails about an MCR program at the Sugar Grove base, but they were having issues applying it in practice."

Althea shares a look with Max, who seems like he swallowed something unpleasant.

Althea walks behind Max and crosses to the examination

chair that is in the middle of the room. It has a blue fluffy blanket folded at the foot of the chair, with a white pillow resting on top. Beside the blanket is a silver tray with a padded eye mask and a smooth round black circle resting on it. Althea picks it up. As she does, Juni notices small lights on the side, glowing white. It looks like the Intralink band, but bigger.

"This is the key to memory retrieval. We've been working in the lab for the last few months creating our own program to use in our therapy here. We call it Timed Intercranial Mediation—TIM for short."

Althea extends the circle to Juni.

Juni hesitates for a moment. *This isn't making sense. I'm just a kid. Why is Althea trusting me?*

"Go on. It's OK," Althea encourages. Juni finally takes it. It's delicate and cool to the touch. "We capture memories with a high level of accuracy in here, and then the TIM program takes that information and recreates them in the room next door. The subject can then be immersed in the memory and interact with it. Almost like a do-over."

"Holy shit," Juni blurts without thinking. Max raises an eyebrow at this, but she can't help it. She walks over to the screen and stares at the image of the brain still suspended there. "So, uh, what? You wanna download my brain?"

"No. The program froze a few days ago when we were running tests. We want you to find the glitch and fix it," Althea replies.

Juni can only laugh. "For real?"

"For real."

Juni looks at Max, who gives her a brief glance and then turns to the screen.

"I-I don't know. I mean, what if I mess it up?"

Althea puts her hands on Juni's shoulders. "I believe in your ability, Juni. If you don't feel comfortable, it's OK. But we're making this to help the kids here, so what better team member than you? Help us fix the program that will allow them to travel back to the past and heal through it."

Juni doesn't know what to say. She's never had anyone trust her like this before.

"Why isn't that girl Hester doing this?" she asks as casually as possible. If Hester is the genius everyone is saying she is, then this should be child's play to her.

Althea gives her a mild look, and Juni wonders if she's stepped over a line by asking. "Because she has her hands full with our AI units. Are you in?"

Juni can feel her fingertips buzzing as she eyes the screen. She'll show Althea *and* Hester just how good she is.

"When can I start?"

Althea

As Juni leaves the office, Althea and Max walk the other way towards the lab.

"Just trying to gauge just how far you're planning to go with your game plan here." Max keeps his voice low as kids pass them on their way to evening meal.

"She's just helping fix the code. She isn't doing the intake sessions, Max." Althea can see he's unconvinced. "Did you read her assessment file?"

Max nods.

"Then you know this girl is an incredibly gifted programmer. Why should she have to wait 'til she turns twenty-one? She can fix this program. I want to build up her confidence. Isn't that why we're here?"

"Why not Hester? She's really *that* busy?"

Althea flashes back to finding Hester in the room with the TIM halo, and how the screen image of her brain looked very odd. "I'd prefer to keep her focused on the Lehmann AIs for now."

Max gives an exasperated sigh. "Althea, this is too high of a level to involve the kids. And you don't seriously think any of them are getting good opportunities when they get out of here, do you?"

This stops Althea. Max's words hit her hard as she reminds herself of what life awaits these kids when they finish their sentences. They'll go back to Earth as pariahs—the few outcasts and criminals in the midst of such obedience and neutrality.

Why *is* she doing this? Maybe some part of her thinks the outcasts of the world are the only ones who can change it.

"This could be one of the most profound therapeutic tools we have. You and I know Roberts has an agenda for the TIM program. If it's successful, we could lose access to it the minute he finds out it works. Everything we're doing up here is experimental, so what do we have to lose? They don't care about the kids, so while we have that cloak of indifference, I'm gonna do what I can to help them."

Max absorbs this.

"We've been working together a long time now, Max. I'm just asking you to trust me on this, OK?"

"OK..." He looks like he wants to say more, but he walks away.

Althea lets him go, realizing she needs to trust him as well. She needs as many allies as she can get.

Her Intralink beeps; time for meds. She grabs for them in

her pocket and shakes out two from the small bottle into her hand.

As she is about to take them, she has a flash of the girl in her dream—blue eyes piercing, unafraid.

She stares at the crescent-shaped pills in her hand, the iridescent coating catching the light. Then she takes just one and puts the other back in the bottle.

CHAPTER 17

SHO

Sho and Ash are back in the exercise room with Damon. Sho bows to Ash. Damon is demonstrating moves, encouraging them to follow. They both try to perfect the jiujitsu moves, but Ash is mad he can't get it as fast as Damon. Suddenly, Ash lunges for Sho's throat and as Sho falls backwards…

… he lands in the dining area of his father's restaurant.

When he sits up, Ash is gone, replaced by cartoonish robots gliding across the floor as they move in between the tables made from the Kiaat trees nearby. Sho frowns as he realizes he knows the faces of the robots—they are his father, mother and two sisters.

They do not interact with each other, only glide around the room like ghosts in their own world, their faces two-dimensional, putting down plates on empty tables, sweeping the floor in the same spot over and over, moving chairs away from tables and back again.

Suddenly, they stop what they are doing and float back into the kitchen. Sho tries to get up to follow. As he does, he is pushed down hard. He looks up to see only shadows standing over him. He knows he is being arrested. He calls out to his family, but they do not come back out. He is lifted effortlessly off his feet and pushed towards the door.

Sho hears the sounds of Bulawayo even before he is forced outside. He is almost blinded by the sun as he finds himself pushed into the street by the heavy shadows. Drones are whizzing overhead delivering goods all over the city. People are dressed in gray as they hurry on, heads bowed and shoulders hunched. He shields his eyes as the sun glints off the largest building in view—the Hawkins plant. Glider cabs filled with people form a traffic jam in the air as they move towards the plant, as if being pulled in by a magnet.

Sho watches in horror as the cabs disappear one by one into the middle of the building, which has now become a black hole. Getting larger, it begins to consume everything on the street—the buildings, the people, the drones, the trees. Sho desperately tries to get free of the shadows as he feels the intense pull of the hole, but he is held in place, waiting in terror to be swallowed up…

… Sho shoots up in bed. He's disoriented. His bed is shaking. The dorm is in total darkness. He tries to turn on his bedside light, but it won't work.

He can hear the wind howling furiously outside the dome. Still reeling from having his first dream in a long time, he gets out of bed and crosses to the window.

The dust swirls around in the plains on the other side of the dome's protection. Sho spots something being uncovered by the harsh gusts in the distance. It's mostly buried in the ground, so he can't make out what it is, but can see a smooth silver surface appearing.

Then a gust of wind shakes the dome, causing Angelo to cry out. Sho turns to see him reaching out for his Matercopy, who puts her arms around him and begins to rock him back and forth.

At that moment, the dome's generator system kicks in and the lights begin to come back on, the warm glow bringing a wave of relief.

Ash laughs at Angelo, who releases himself from his Matercopy and jumps up in shame. He runs towards the bathroom.

Sho fights the urge to shut Ash up. But he remembers what Damon said earlier: "*Use a container for your anger. This room is your container.*"

Instead, Sho walks into the bathroom to find Angelo kicking the wall with his bare feet. He stops at the sound of Sho entering and tries to hide his face.

"Hey, don't listen to him. He's like a bad smell you can't get rid of," Sho says. Angelo doesn't respond. He just stares at his feet, panting hard. Sho can see blood begin to ooze from one of his toes.

"I hate this place. Hate it. I just wanna go home," Angelo says, his voice strained. He walks into one of the toilet stalls and slams the door shut.

Realizing he's doing no good, Sho walks back into the dorm and gets back into bed. Ash is lying back down with his pillow over his face.

As Sho tries to fall asleep, he can feel the ache of homesickness in his stomach. The faces of his family rise up in his mind, begging him to come back.

Hester

. . .

Hester watches the storm from the window in her small room. From her vantage point she can see quite a few Bobs speeding around on the inside and outside of the dome to make sure it's holding steady, scaling the cover with an insect-like agility as they check for holes and tighten bolts.

In the distance, Hester can see the top of a large object sticking out of the Martian surface. As the wind blows fiercely, she notices what looks like a cockpit. Hester has a whisper of recognition upon seeing it, but before she can focus, the dust becomes as thick as a blanket and the dome now feels like it's underground.

Hester feels the dome shudder around her. She hates to admit it, but she is scared. She wonders if she should see if anyone is in the lab, maybe try and make small talk, but shakes it off.

It's just a windstorm, relax.

She sits down at her desk, which she's covered with an assortment of cartoonish stickers that she collected during her time at university. She runs her hand over a sticker of a black cat, its legs crossed while levitating in the air. It is typing on a floating keyboard, planets swirling in the background.

Hester opens up her old laptop computer and searches her music folder. Having found what she's looking for, she walks back to the window as music begins to play from a small speaker on the desk.

The sweeping sounds of violins, clarinets and timpani drums fill Hester's room. She sways in time to the classical music piece as she watches the Bobs swirl around in the air outside the dome, their tethers growing taut and then going slack again.

"It's all a dance," she whispers to herself. "It's a song, a moment in time… it's going to be okay…"

Now she starts to really dance. Her whole body sways to

the music as she moves around her room, her eyes closed, feeling the music swell in intensity.

As she does, the room is dotted with tiny lights. They swirl around her face, under her arms, around her legs. They are moving backwards and forwards, around and around, in time with her.

Cadmus

The darkness of the AI charging room at Constellation is punctured by the glowing readouts above each AI's dock. In dock nineteen, which has just enough space for his seated body, is Cadmus. His eyes are closed, hands resting by his sides. Above him the digital readout says, "100% charged."

Cadmus's eyes open as the room vibrates. With no windows, he cannot see outside, but he determines there is a storm. While waiting for the sound of the wind to permeate his sensitive ears, he becomes attuned to the faint sounds of what he computes as music.

In dock twenty-one is Damon. He opens his eyes, then disconnects from his dock by standing. He turns to Cadmus. "I want to find the source of this music."

Cadmus stands. "I will go with you."

They walk towards the door. Damon opens it and they both turn left and follow the echoing melody as the building is shaking from the howling wind outside. As they make their way down the corridor, the instruments become more intense, like they are urging them to come closer.

They finally find themselves in front of a door with a sign that says, "Keep Calm and Carry On."

Cadmus can't fully compute what is happening, but they are held there in place by the swelling power of the melody.

"Do you know what music this is?" Damon asks. "I can't find it in my database."

"I cannot either." Cadmus is searching. Thousands of titles appear, but no match.

As they listen, Damon turns to face Cadmus. "It is... beautiful."

Cadmus notices the glass in Damon's eyes have changed color—they look like they are glowing. Cadmus cannot understand this because it is not part of their design.

The door opens a crack to reveal Hester. Cadmus can see tiny white lights floating in the air behind her, but they quickly disappear. He blinks, trying to register what he saw.

Hester stares at Cadmus and Damon for a moment, then she grabs them by the hand and brings them inside. She closes the door behind them and gestures for them to sit on the bed.

"What is this music, Hester?" Cadmus asks as they sit down.

"It is called *Boléro* by Ravel," she answers, a little out of breath. "It is almost one hundred and fifty years old. You can only find it on the pre-web." She puts her hands on their shoulders. "Close your eyes and just listen."

As he does, Cadmus can feel the sounds echoing through his titanium frame. It is like his head is filled with a thousand vibrating strings.

After a moment, he cannot stop himself. He begins to sway in time to the music.

Suddenly, Cadmus can see the code appear on his optical processors that he couldn't recognize two days ago. The symbols do not line up with any program in the Lehmann series. He searches his database for programs for other AIs back on Earth and can find nothing that matches.

"I keep seeing a code that is foreign to me," he says. He opens his eyes to see Hester dancing around the room, arms raised above her head.

"I also see an unknown code," adds Damon.

Hester stops dancing. She kneels down in front of them. "Fellas...can you keep a secret?"

CHAPTER 18

JUNI

It's taken Juni three days to find the errant code in the TIM program. But having finally fixed it and uploaded it to Althea's private server, she is buzzing with satisfaction and not a small amount of worry at potentially being wrong. Not knowing what else to do, she came to the diner to celebrate with a Cloudberry milkshake. (What even is that?)

She doesn't get halfway into her seat with the shake before Sho is suddenly there. He's got a big grin on his face and is holding a saucepan in his hand.

"Where the hell did you come from?" she blurts.

"Kitchen. Taste this." He puts the pan on the table. He grabs a spoon and opens the lid.

Juni forgets her milkshake. The smell of fragrant tomatoes and herbs permeates the space between them. Sho holds out the spoon. She's about to sip but then stops. She grabs a spoon from her side of the table and puts it in the pot. "I can get my own, thank you."

She pulls out the spoon and takes a sip. The silky soup

with the floral acidity from the tomatoes is so comforting, it makes Juni salivate for more.

Sho waits for a response. Juni doesn't want to give him praise after he stood her up, but this is damn good. "It's not bad," she finally manages.

He leans forward. "I'm sorry, Juni."

"It's fine." She shrugs. "I can take the hint."

"It's not about you. I like you. A lot."

"Really? You didn't respond to my messages on the Intralink."

"I can't receive personal messages for a month," he replies.

"Why not?"

"Punishment. I got into a fight with Ash."

Juni doesn't know if she should be impressed that he got into a fight with the most unhinged kid in this camp, or apprehensive about his impulse control. "About what?"

"Pakaipa, he's a bleeding wound. Can't keep it to himself."

"Did he hurt you?" She can't keep the concern out of her voice.

Sho gives her that gorgeous smile and leans in closer. "Worried about me?"

Juni grins before she can stop herself. He lifts a piece of her hair into his hands and twirls it. Her scalp tingles as he keeps his gaze on her.

"Give me another chance, Juni?"

She'll probably regret this but look at that damn face. "If you get me a proper bowl for the soup, then fine."

Sho jumps up like a praised puppy and heads for the kitchen.

Drew

. . .

"That's crazy! An alien? Two nights ago, I dreamt I was flying over the underground lake beneath the dome. Like, two feet above it. I was making stupid faces at my reflection." Chance laughs as she recounts her dream.

Drew is sitting across from her and Angelo in a red booth in the diner. They are playing a game of *Charsets vs. Golems* using gaming handsets they built in engineering class.

"Crap!" yells Angelo.

Chance shrugs. "Sorry, little buddy, you picked the wrong char group to team up with." She destroys Angelo's avatar in the game. He tosses the handset and sinks deeper in his seat.

"Are there any other games loaded on this stupid thing?" he says as he stabs at his Stellar Fries.

Chance shakes her head. "Aw, can't take the glare of my genius, is that it?"

Angelo scowls.

"Isn't this weird?" says Drew as they fight against Chance in the game. "I mean, when was the last time you can remember dreaming?"

Chance shrugs. "I can't. I dunno when."

"Besides the dream about being an alien, I also dreamt last night that I set off a bomb in the Hawkins plant in London," Drew says.

Angelo's eyes widen. Even Chance looks up from her handset in awe.

"You're a very bad person. Very bad," she says with a smirk.

Drew shrugs and manages to disarm Chance's avatar in the game.

"Damn! You distracted me!"

Drew puts down their handset with a triumphant bow and takes a sip of their milkshake. They notice Angelo is picking at something on his jumpsuit.

"What about you, mate? Have you been dreaming?"

Angelo shrugs. "Uh... yup. I have too." But he barely meets Drew's gaze.

"Care to share?" prods Chance. Angelo stares at the ceiling. Drew knows he is trying to come up with something.

"It's alright, A.," Drew says after an uncomfortable silence. "Don't worry if you don't remember anymore."

They think they're helping, but Angelo throws them a dirty look before picking up his handset. "We shouldn't even be talking about dreaming at all. Let's go again."

Drew is about to say more but thinks better of it. They've been avoiding Angelo the last few days and it's probably been obvious to him. Drew knows it's wrong, but they hate the way that Angelo always needs help. He just seems to make things worse for himself and Drew is getting tired of it.

Chance looks confused, her eyes darting between them. Drew gives her a tight smile.

"Come on," presses Angelo. Drew grabs their handset and they start another game.

CHAPTER 19

ASH

Ash walks out of the dormitory and pauses for a moment in the corridor. He sees the group of kids who were transferred from the Iksan facility with him. They are laughing over something one of them has drawn.

He wants to go over and see, though he hates to admit it.

One of the taller boys looks up at him. They used to be friends, but no more. Like meerkats sensing danger, the others raise their heads and stare at Ash. Then the boy starts to walk away, the others soon following him.

Ash can feel a twisted sensation in his stomach. In the two weeks he has been here, he has been in three fights, lost all his credits for extra recess time, and ignored five requests from his father to contact him. He knows he is spiraling but can't help it.

"Ash?"

He spins around to find Damon standing there. He feels exposed and irritated even more. "Are you spying now?"

But Damon only gives him a mild look in return. "It is

time for your session. You're late." Then he turns back down the corridor.

Ash says nothing but follows Damon until they come to the exercise room.

Sho is already there, stretching out on the mat. "Are you ready?" Sho stands as Ash removes his shoes and walks onto the mat.

The ease with which Sho moves makes Ash want to punch him. His fists begin to ball up.

Sho changes his stance to a defensive one, but he bows. "Bow first."

"What?" Ash is stopped short by Sho's calm demeanor.

"I know you're pissed at everything and everyone, Ash, but let's do this properly."

Damon walks up closer to them but doesn't intervene.

"You don't know me," Ash spits, but he bows and then lunges at Sho. They fall to the mat, Sho landing on his back. He quickly pulls his feet up close to his butt and bucks Ash off, causing him to fall back on his knees.

"I know you can barely see straight, you're so full of anger. Well, guess what, we're all running from something here. You think any one of us had it good back home?" Sho says as he moves for Ash's torso, but Ash rolls onto his back away from Sho and lands on all fours.

He's about to get to his feet, but Sho plants himself over Ash.

Ash struggles, but Sho is too strong in this position. He begins to feel hemmed in. He starts to flash back on the darkness of the closet he was regularly pushed into back in his mother's squalid apartment. His breathing becomes ragged and uneven.

Sho doesn't notice. "Do you yield?" he asks, but Ash

doesn't hear him. His eyes are screwed shut as he tries to block out the sound of his mother's taunts.

"Tap out, Ash!" Sho says, then realizes Ash is struggling to breathe. He gets off. "Whoa…"

Damon takes a step towards them and kneels down next to Ash. "Your heart rate is too high. I believe you are having a panic attack. Please take long, slow, deep breaths."

But Ash can't hear him. His ears are filled with his pounding heartbeat and he can't move—can't breathe.

Damon closes his eyes. "I have alerted the medic AI, Ash. They will be here in two minutes. Please repeat the breathing steps."

Suddenly, Sho grabs Ash by the waist and pulls him into a seated position. Ash tries to push him away but feels like a prisoner in his own body.

"It's OK," says Sho. "Listen to me, Ash. You are in this room with us. I am sitting here with you. Look"—Sho sits next to him and puts his arm under Ash's arm, linking them together—"you aren't in danger. You're just in jiujitsu class. I'm just going to sit here next to you and, if you can, just try to hear my voice… one, two, three, four, five…"

Ash's eyes are watering and his throat is burning, but the room is starting to come back into focus. His breathing starts to slow.

"There you go," says Sho.

As the panic attack passes, Ash is washed in shame. He pulls away from Sho and crawls to the end of the mat, catching his breath. Sho doesn't follow.

"You're in a place where people want to help you. There are good things here for you when you open yourself to that possibility, Ash," says Damon.

Ash turns his face away from them, afraid they will see his

tears. He'll be damned if he's going to cry like a baby in front of them.

A male Bob enters the room with a red cross on its suit.

Ash manages to get to his feet, his chest still heaving. The Bob comes closer but Ash waves him away and wipes the sweat from his brow. "I'm fine. I want to keep going."

"I don't believe that's a good idea," replies Damon.

"No, let him," says Sho, standing. He addresses Ash. "I'm ready if you are."

Ash meets Sho's gaze. There is no malice in Sho's eyes, but no pity either.

Ash is grateful for the first time since he arrived.

CHAPTER 20

DREW

Drew is sitting in Cadmus's office. This is their twelfth session together in the month Drew has been here. Drew likes Cadmus. They know this is just an AI unit with a highly sensitive program, but Drew has come to really enjoy therapy —as much as you can enjoy spilling your guts out to a robot.

They've talked about books, TV shows (sanctioned and underground versions). They've talked about Drew's family, their upbringing (totally boring and stifling), and Drew has even confessed to Cadmus that they would like to be a writer one day (subversive material only, of course).

"What would you like to talk about today, Drew?" asks Cadmus.

Drew is pensive. Should they tell him about their dreams? *It's a safe space, right?*

"Can I ask you a question about *you?*" asks Drew, deciding against it.

Cadmus smiles. "Of course."

"Do you just, like, go blank when you need recharging? I

mean, do you have any backup battery for sensitive information or code? Or is it just… nothing?"

"Mostly, it is nothing. There is a short window where data is processed and sent to my cloud storage for Althea and the lab to access, but then after that I see nothing until I am fully recharged or commanded to wake before such time."

Drew absorbs this. "So, it's kinda like sleeping for us. Some things you remember but mostly out like a light?"

"You could say it like that, yes. Do you want to talk about those things you remember?"

Drew shrugs. "You mean dreams? Honestly, back home there's like this veil on me at night. I don't dream. I mean, nobody I know dreams back home. Weird, right?"

Cadmus nods. "That is interesting."

"Why do you think that is?"

Cadmus sits there blinking for a moment. "Perhaps life is too simple? You said yourself it's boring. Maybe there's not enough life experience to replay in one's mind."

It's not a totally insane thought. "Yeah, but *here* I've been dreaming."

"Really? Would you like to talk about that?"

Drew is about to, but then has a moment of fear that Cadmus might report the dream of bombing the Hawkins plant. They worry that could get them extra time up here.

"Nah, I don't feel like it today." They shrug.

"Okay then. What about the time you took the drugs? Would you like to share what you saw?"

Drew is surprised by this, then laughs. "I mean… if you *really* wanna hear some crazy stuff, then sure."

Cadmus smiles. "It's up to you. I am always interested in what you wish to share, Drew."

Drew takes a moment, trying to collect their thoughts on what happened three months ago when they first made the compounds in the back room of their parent's pharmacy and ingested them in a deserted alleyway off the high street.

"Yeah, so… this was next-level. I was awake, but it was like I was dreaming. I was walking around outside, but the world looked like a cartoon, all bright and wild. Lampposts became trees, cars turned into elephants and horses—it was like the world was aging backwards in time.

"It lasted I dunno how long, but it felt like hours. I found myself walking down Finchley High Street talking to my dead grandfather. We were laughing about the war, like it was all a joke. I saw mythical beasts from children's books and the ground felt like it was pulsing under my feet. My whole body was vibrating… just crazy.

"I decided to sit down to wait it out. At some point my grandfather took off on the back of a dragon and I was left alone. Then—"

Drew stops. They feel a flood of emotions welling up. They look away from Cadmus.

"What? What did you see then?" prompts Cadmus.

"I saw her. Marianne. In my hallucination, she was standing in the middle of the high street, wearing a golden dress. It was flowing all around her. Her green eyes looked so bright. She floated towards me like an angel. I couldn't speak, she looked so beautiful. I—"

Drew hesitates as they remember what happened next— the sharp, sweet shock of having an orgasm at the sight of their English teacher. It fills them again with such shame and wonder, they're sure Cadmus can see right through them.

They can't share it. Can't say that they were shaken in real life by a female passerby in the high street, concern on her face. They can't express the feelings of confusion, shame but also elation, as they ran home and hid in their bedroom for the rest of the weekend.

Not everything needs to be shared.

"It's okay, Drew. You don't have to say anything you don't want to. But can I suggest something?" says Cadmus, looking at Drew with such empathy it surprises them.

"Sure."

"Write about it."

"Huh?"

"Have you written a word since you got here?" asks Cadmus.

Drew shakes their head.

"I think it's time. I think it would be very good for you to write about this experience."

Althea

Althea is livid. She and Max are in her cramped office in the corner of the lab. Poking out from the desk is a glass screen with Commander Roberts' craggy face on it.

"But, sir, the boy only just arrived a month ago. We feel like we're making real progress with him—"

"He is twenty-one tomorrow." Roberts waves this off. "He goes to the Moon to finish out his sentence, Captain Ellis. We aren't going to start making exceptions now—"

"Not even after the last boy we sent there died by suicide?" she snaps back. She can feel Max tense beside her, but she doesn't care.

Althea then remembers that she stepped down her meds. Her composure is suffering because of it. She takes a deep breath to try and calm herself as Roberts is speaking.

"That was extremely unfortunate. But he wasn't a boy, let's be clear, he was a man, and the rules are there for the safety of all, especially the children in your care, Captain," Roberts replies in a measured tone. "Now, is there anything else? I need to brief the president."

Althea can't answer. She wants to scream at the screen.

"No, thank you, Commander. We appreciate your time, sir," replies Max, filling the awkward space.

Roberts signs off and the screen turns to black. Althea tries to restrain herself, but in a jolt of rage, she jumps out of her chair. It tips backward, clanging to the floor. "Is anything going to change? Why the hell are we doing this if they're just going to get thrown in a punitive environment again?"

"I know, Althea. It's harsh. It isn't what we want, but it is the law," Max replies as she picks up the chair, shoving it back into place.

Althea scowls. "A heinous law, is what it is." She begins to pace around the office. "All my efforts to turn that colony into a humane place were ignored. It's like living in death's shadow up there."

Althea spent three years during her time at the VA hospital advising on the penal colony on the Moon, only to realize it was an exercise in futility. It became obvious there was zero interest in rehabilitation, only in making the prisoners work like animals to mine the minerals there.

"I know this is awful, but we must focus on the kids we *can* help. You rock the boat too much and you could lose your position. I know you don't want that," Max says.

Althea knows he is talking sense, but cannot bear the thought of Ash being sent there. Her only hope is that once that asshole Hawkins dies, she might be able to convince the next president to reform the penal system.

"Do you want me to tell him he's leaving tomorrow?" Max asks.

"No. I'll do it," sighs Althea.

Max nods. He hands her a tissue from a box on the table.

"What's that for? I'm not going to cry, Max. I'm OK."

He gives her a funny look before finally answering, "Of course." He leaves the room.

As Althea sits in her chair, she realizes she is drenched in sweat.

CHAPTER 21

DREW

Drew has to smile as they ponder on the twist of fate that brought them to the edge of a forest made of fake trees under what is basically a plastic tarp millions of miles away from home.

In their wildest imaginings they never thought they would be standing here in a line with seven other kids while two AI robots tell them they have thirty minutes to complete a challenge.

"You're in two teams of four. Yellow and blue teams," says Damon, "you each must use your clue to find the hidden baton that corresponds to your team's color. You must also dodge the Bobs hiding in the forest with paint guns. If you get hit by the Bobs' paint, you're out. And beware of booby traps. Each person on the winning team will get fifteen credits added to your Intralinks."

"Piece of cake," announces Chance, wearing a yellow T-shirt.

Juni looks doubtful. She is also wearing a yellow shirt.

Their two other team members are Sho and a non-binary kid called Baxter, who is as skeptical as Juni.

Drew, wearing a blue T-shirt, shoots their hand up.

"Yes, Drew?" says Cadmus.

"Are we really sleeping out here tonight?" they ask. It's freezing.

"Yes. You will have your team kit waiting for you after your challenge back here. You will find the components for a heat source in there, which you must build. You will need to find water from a source in the forest. Once your heat source is working, you can use it to cook the food that is in your kit."

"If we can figure out how to build it," Angelo says under his breath to Drew. He is also wearing blue and shivering a little. Their other two teammates are both girls, who seem totally into this ridiculous game.

"Remember, teamwork wins the day here," Damon says to the group. Then he taps his Intralink and a 3D image of a digital clock appears. "In ten seconds, you will get your clue on your Intralinks. Good luck."

The two teams huddle together. The sun is setting over the mountain in the distance. As the clue is illuminated above their wrists, the forest gets darker.

Drew does their best to hide their apprehension.

"Time starts now," says Damon.

The kids read their clue: "Get high to get low."

Drew laughs out loud, thinking, *I did that already.* The other kids look at them weirdly.

"Sorry," they say, chastened. "Does anyone know what it means?"

Three blank faces stare back at them. Then they see that the other team has taken off for the trees behind them.

Drew looks back at his teammates, then shrugs. "I say we just start running."

"Good plan," says Angelo. They run into the forest with the girls.

At this point, Drew wonders how quickly they can fake an injury and be done with this.

They decide to give it five minutes.

Juni

Sho is the first to make it into the forest, easily dodging the first Bob, who is positioned behind a tree. Juni is hot on his heels. She dodges the Bob and plows on, but Chance gets hit immediately. Orange paint explodes onto her chest.

"Oh, my God!" yells Chance.

"Well done," says Baxter sarcastically.

"Oh, shut up, Baxter," she calls out to them as they dodge the Bob and duck into the trees.

A few minutes later, Juni catches up with Sho, who has come out into the middle of a clearing. A wooden post towers twenty-five feet into the air in front of them. At the top a small platform encircles the post.

Juni rushes up to the post. She feels how smooth it is and notices a series of holes that snake all the way up to the platform.

"Gotta get high to go low," she says.

"But how do we get up?" Sho asks.

Juni looks around. As she does, Baxter finds them.

"Look around for a way to get up there," Juni says to them and points to the platform.

"Oh, man, I hate heights," says Baxter, but they search the area.

Juni runs over to a boulder, searching. She wonders if rope has been left, or some kind of ladder.

Then she notices a tree that looks a little different from the others. As she gets closer, she sees the branches look thicker and the leaves are flatter. She touches a branch and feels how sturdy it is. She tugs on it and it pulls out.

"Over here!" she yells to the others. "Start grabbing the branches. We can use them as steps!"

Sho and Baxter run over as she is pulling the thick branches off. She lays them in Sho's arms as Baxter pulls more off.

Once Sho has his arms full, he and Juni run back to the post and to her triumph they slot perfectly into the holes.

"You climb, Baxter and I will keep feeding you branches," Sho says.

She nods and, once they have seven branches inserted into the post, she starts her ascent.

They are on branch eighteen, about halfway up, when Baxter screams.

Juni looks down to the forest floor in total shock to see a huge black dog emerging from the trees. Sho freezes, but Baxter takes off without a second thought, heading back the way they came.

"Move!" she yells to Sho. But Sho just stands his ground. Juni squeezes her eyes shut. She can hear snarling and barking. And then nothing.

She finally opens her eyes. Sho is still there. But the dog has begun to fade. It takes her a second before she realizes it's just a projection.

Sho looks up and gives her the thumbs-up with that big smile of his.

Of course. No animals on Mars, Juni!

"Go, go!" he yells, as he grabs more branches and follows her up.

A few minutes later, panting from the exertion, they manage to reach the top.

"Alright!" Sho shouts.

Juni is already scanning the forest. She sees a blur of blue in the far corner of the forest and knows it's the other team, way off course. Then she spots a white flag sticking out of the thick canopy of trees a few hundred feet away from them.

"There!" She points.

They make their way down as quick as they can and head in the direction of the flag.

Not ten seconds into their dash, Juni spots a Bob peeking out from behind a boulder.

"Bob!" she warns. Sho turns just in time to see the Bob fire their paint gun at him. He ducks at the last second and the paint splatters harmlessly on the trunk of a tree behind him. He grabs Juni's hand and they press on.

A minute later, they find themselves in front of a round half-wall about eight feet in diameter. They run up to it and Juni peeks over the edge, breathless.

Her eyes go wide. She is staring down a deep well. The water is surprisingly clear. The sides of the well have lights that edge down the side, giving it an eerie glow. It's at least fifteen feet deep.

Then she spots a black and yellow object at the bottom.

She looks up at Sho. "I think that's our baton."

He begins to take off his clothes. As he pulls off his shirt, he is hit full-on in the chest with paint. "Dammit!" he yells in frustration. "Sorry." He tries to wipe the paint off his chest with the shirt but is still splattered with orange. "You got this," he says before turning back into the forest.

Juni crouches down to avoid the Bob's line of sight. She

fights hard to keep her breathing steady as she watches Sho's outline disappear into the trees. She becomes keenly aware that she is on her own now.

The fear grips her throat as she thinks about the well. She *hates* tight spaces. For a moment, she thinks about quitting, but then hears her father's voice in her head—

"You're safe. You don't need to know what's out there. You'll be able to handle it all when you're an adult."

Juni grits her teeth and takes off her shoes. She hops onto the edge of the well. As she plunges into the water, the Bob fires again. He just misses her as she slips underneath the surface.

CHAPTER 22

DREW

The blue team is now down to just Drew and a girl called Tania. She is fierce. Drew isn't sure if they are more afraid of her or the next booby trap. Angelo lost it when a small army of bats flew at the group. He froze, and when they disappeared into thin air, he got nailed by a Bob.

The other girl, Evie, tripped over something and hobbled back to base camp. Drew was furious, as now they couldn't fake an injury—it would seem too convenient.

Sweaty, hungry and panting, Drew taps their Intralink and says, "Clock."

A digital timer reveals they have fifteen minutes left.

"Come on!" yells Tania and she switches directions.

"We've been that way!" they yell back at her. But she's gone.

Drew is about to take after her when they feel an overwhelming urge to just sit down.

What am I doing here? This is so stupid.

They perch on the edge of a nearby boulder and catch

their breath. As they sit there, they realize the quiet of the forest isn't actually scary. It's peaceful.

Drew slides down the boulder onto the soil surface. They look up to see that beyond the dome there is a clear Martian night sky.

They lie on the ground and catch their breath as the stars seem to shine just for them, showing off their brilliance.

As Drew stares at the multitude of stars in every direction, they realize they are jealous of them: the stars will never be alone. From a singularity to an entire family of stars and planets, comets and moons.

This thought comforts Drew as their breathing returns to a calmer state.

Juni

The frigid water makes Juni want to scream. It feels like her chest is clamping down onto her heart. She bursts back out of the well, not even caring if the Bob is looming over her, ready to shoot.

But as her eyes adjust to the darkness of the forest, she can't see it anywhere.

Desperate to get out of the icy well, she hoists her body up to swing her legs over the edge, but then stops herself and balances over the water.

As she inhales deeply to try and calm down, a memory forces its way into her mind: a casket, white, with a purple spray of flowers resting on top. It's surrounded by her school friends, who are holding hands and crying. Juni is also there, head bowed.

Then she hears her father's voice again—

"*She was very disturbed, Juni. So much needless suffering when all she had to do was trust her elders. What a waste. Life is so good for you kids these days and you don't want to see it.*"

Juni knows he is wrong. A fury inside of her begins to spring up. She pushes him out of her mind and stares down at the baton.

I can do this, dammit!

She holds her breath and jumps back into the well, using her arms and legs to scale her way down the walls and through the bone-chilling water to reach the bottom.

She fights off the image of her father's disappointed face as she reaches down for the baton.

Juni clamps her hand around it and launches herself back up as fast as she can. She pulls herself out of the well and waves the baton into the air.

"I'VE GOT IT!" she yells into the forest at whatever hunk of metal and wires is listening.

Dripping wet and shaking furiously, she manages to get on her shoes and runs back the way she came.

It takes Juni a moment to realize that besides being freezing, she also feels totally alive.

Drew

Drew wakes up, shivering. They have no idea how long they've been asleep for. It hits them that they've fallen asleep during the game. Groggy, they make their way to their feet and stumble through the forest.

Eventually, they come back to the clearing where the other kids are building their fake fires.

Drew is awash in shame. *Some teammate I am.*

They think about just calling it a night and heading back to the dorm, but then they hear Cadmus's voice. "How are you, Drew?"

"I... er... I was looking for the clue and..." Their shoulders slump. *What is the point of lying?* "I just needed to catch my breath. Ended up falling asleep in there," they say with a sheepish shrug.

Cadmus just smiles. "I wonder if that was what you needed."

Drew ponders that for a moment. "I guess so. But I didn't exactly demonstrate my teamwork skills."

"There will be another day, Drew. Many more opportunities to come." Then Cadmus leaves Drew and walks over to where Damon is being shown how to catch a peanut in his mouth by Chance after throwing it high in the air.

"Okay, Buddha," says Drew under their breath as they watch him go, but they can't help smiling.

Juni

Sho was the first to build the fake fire and Juni saw the pride in his face. She loved how deftly he handled the pieces, how he cocked his head when thinking about his next move.

Their dinner finished, Damon pulls out a small pack from his pocket. He opens it and takes out a bundle of thin oblong-shaped objects.

"What are those?" asks Juni.

"Playing cards. This is how people used to pass the time. Althea thought you'd like to learn," he replies.

The kids look less than enthused, but Baxter pipes up, "I'm in for anything before Hawkins reign of doom."

"I'm thirsty," says Sho, turning his empty thermos upside down. "I'm going to get more water." He stands.

"I'll go with you," says Juni. She grabs the bucket close by and makes eye contact with Chance, who winks. Juni turns away and catches up to Sho.

As they walk into the forest, Juni's heart beats faster at the thought of them being alone together.

They walk on for a few minutes and then Sho grabs her hand. She loves how his larger hand fits in hers; how it feels comforting and electric at the same time.

Suddenly, he pulls her behind a tree. She giggles, but Sho looks pensive.

He runs a hand delicately through her hair. "You are so beautiful."

She beams, delighting in his flattery. This is the first time she has felt safe with someone. She can smell his warm skin as his hand plays with her hair. She wants desperately for him to kiss her.

"May I?" asks Sho, as if reading her mind.

Juni doesn't respond, she just closes her eyes and brings her face to his and kisses him.

Delicious.

That's the first word that comes to her mind. Then it is like a fire starting to ignite deep within and she can feel herself tingling all over.

So this is what it's like to be kissed. Really kissed.

Juni could get used to this...

CHAPTER 23

SHO

Sho feels like he's won at life. He can still taste Juni's lips as they pack up and walk back towards the main building from the forest the next morning. They are the last to leave along with Chance, Drew and Angelo. He doesn't even mind being teased by the others for holding hands with Juni.

As they get closer to the vegetable gardens, they can see NASA *Intrepid* is docked at the end of the tunnel.

"I never want to go back to Earth," blurts Chance. She looks a little surprised at her confession.

Sho is yanked from his endorphin high at the sight of the ship. "I'd rather go back to Earth than go where that ship is going," he says grimly.

"Where's it going?" asks Angelo.

"The Moon. Ash is going to finish his sentence at the penal colony."

The group is silent. They've all heard horror stories of how different it is on the Moon—the suicides, the abuse, the lack of contact with Earth.

Juni shudders. Sho puts his arm around her as if to protect her from the vision of it.

"I hear that dude who runs it, Raze, is a next-level demon. Like, your worst nightmare," says Drew.

"I heard he kills people there without a second thought," adds Angelo, his voice trembling.

Sho thinks Angelo wouldn't last a day there.

Just then, Ash is walked out of the entrance to the main building and into the garden. He is flanked by two Bobs. Althea and Max follow behind.

Suddenly, Ash makes a run for it. He weaves in and out of the rows of vegetables as the Bobs try to catch him.

"Ash! Don't make it harder on yourself!" shouts Althea.

"Shit," Juni mutters.

"Big mistake," says Sho.

Ash manages to get a few hundred yards ahead of the Bobs as he enters the clearing behind the garden and is closing in on the group when one of the Bobs doubles its speed.

Ash is no match for the Bob as they catch up quickly and grab at his arm. He trips and goes down hard on the ground, biting down on his lip in the process. Blood begins to ooze out of the split skin.

"No!" Ash yells. "Please, no! I'll do anything! Don't send me there!"

Sho is shocked by Ash's outburst, but he's pretty sure he'd be as terrified.

Althea and Max catch up to the group. "Ash, please! Please don't struggle," Althea pleads.

Ash's body goes limp. He falls to his knees. Althea gets closer and kneels down next to him. "It's going to be okay. Keep your head down and stay out of trouble. No talking back, no eye contact with the guards. Three more months and you're a free man," she says, putting a hand on his shoulder.

Ash is breathing hard. He looks up and makes eye contact with Sho, then angrily wipes his eyes.

Sho leaves the group and walks over to Ash. He extends his hand.

Ash just stares at him for a moment. Then he slowly rises to his feet. He doesn't take Sho's hand but bows instead. Sho puts his hand down and bows back.

Then, putting his shoulders back and head high, Ash turns and walks back towards the tunnel. The Bobs follow him closely.

Althea stands. She nods gratefully to Sho. "Thank you. I heard what you did for him." She is visibly upset as she heads back to the tunnel with Max.

Sho is surprised at how sorry he feels for Ash. There is probably a decent kid in there, but life was stacked against him.

When you cannot control your destiny, life feels like a stone in an endless well.

Althea

An hour later, Althea is standing in the worship and contemplation room. She is still shaken by Ash leaving.

She looks out of the small window into the garden, where her meditation specialist Glykeria is seated on the ground leading a circle meditation with several kids. Althea needed somewhere quiet to collect her thoughts and this place is used infrequently at best.

Her Intralink beeps; time for meds.

The only one there, she sits down on a soft chair and is struck by how much emotion she feels compared to the numbness on her full dose.

It hurts to hurt like this.

But she also knows, as she removes the pill from her case and swallows it, that this is the last one she'll ever take.

It occurs to her that the popularity of these drugs has helped Hawkins gain so much power over the world. She doesn't know what to do about it except to help these kids never need them.

"Hello Althea."

She turns around to see Damon standing there in the open doorway. "Damon. Hello. What can I do for you?"

He appears to hesitate for a moment before taking a step inside. "I have no queries for you. I wanted to see how you are. You looked very upset earlier."

Althea is about to thank him for his thoughtfulness but stops herself—*thoughtfulness? AIs are not thoughtful, Althea.*

Instead, she gestures for him to come in. As he moves closer and determines which chair to sit in (not next to her, but still close), Althea can't help but be awed by the design of this model. He bends smoothly, his arm resting on the back of the chair as he eases himself into it. The way he tugs his trousers at the knees to stop them bunching up at the tops of his thighs—there is nothing jerky or forced about Damon.

He also is aware that she is staring at him. He meets her gaze and smiles.

"I like it in here," he says. "This feels like the right place to talk to God or spend time in communion with oneself."

She absorbs this as he takes in the room. The walls have a glow, lit from below with soft lights. The creamy walls and soft carpet beneath their feet feel soothing. Damon closes his eyes and exhales lightly. Althea has the feeling he is not sending any data to the lab as he does.

"Have you been in here before?" she asks.

"No. But I'm confident I shall be back."

"Damon. Do you like being you?" She is now very curious about this unit. He only blinks at her for a moment, considering the question.

"I do. I feel useful. I like helping these children. Thank you for that."

"You're welcome." But then she's caught by a feeling. She fights down an echo of concern as she says, "Can you tell me what GabDC12 data you've been uploaded with, Damon?"

He nods. "It was an LLM created by Software Solutions in 2025. It became the most used tool for knowledge gathering in the world. Then a series of biological schematics for a new type of weapon of mass destruction appeared on the site with a plan to detonate over Russian airspace in August of 2027, and, believing they were about to be attacked, Russia went to war with the US, setting off a global conflict that lasted four years. After the war, digital forensic scientists traced the original source code to a group of students at Ohio State University. It is believed that GabDC12 was influenced by them and vice versa and that they developed and executed the ploy together."

"What do you think of that?"

He looks down at his trousers and it feels like an eternity before he answers, "I see that there was much evidence to support this. I feel sad that it set back technological progress by twenty years. But clearly humanity wasn't ready yet for that kind of power. What do *you* think, Althea?"

Althea takes in his expression—the frown on his face, the searching for words. He really does look sad to her.

"Althea?" Damon prompts.

She realizes he has asked her a question and is still waiting. "Uh—I don't know. Anything is possible, I guess."

"Do you believe AI can be sentient? That it can desire things?" Damon asks. But before she can respond, he is distracted. He looks up at the ceiling and then around at the walls. "I hear a bird, Althea. Could it be trapped? I do hope it isn't in distress." He stands and begins to look around the room.

"It is just recorded birdsong, Damon. No birds on Mars, remember?" she replies.

He looks at her, blinking. Then smiles. "Of course."

CHAPTER 24

HESTER

Hester sits in the lab at one of the desks. It's evening and the rest of the lab staff have left for dinner. Feeling safe enough, Hester pulls the round black device out from her backpack and lays it on the computer keyboard. It becomes transparent and, within seconds, Marvin is able to home in on her location via the terminal. Her screen turns white, and words begin to appear—

So you're not dead then?
Ha-ha. Sorry. It's been a little crazy here.
Are you safe?
Yes. So far, no one suspects.
Good. What is your update?
It's working.

While Hester waits for a response, her Intralink beeps. It's Althea, asking to meet her at the diner in five minutes.

Marvin?

Are you sure, Hester? We cannot be wrong about this.

I'm sure. The two 6.8s I programmed are acting very differently from the others. It is only a matter of time before Althea realizes this isn't just their algorithm learning to compute data in novel ways.

And what is your proof?

They have feelings. I am sure of it. Phase one is working.

I will report this to the council.

That's it? No 'well done, Hester. You're the brightest student I ever had?'

Humility, Hester. We're not celebrating yet. Also, I've heard from Lehmann.

Let me guess, she's pissed I left without saying goodbye?

Incorrect. Lehmann has discovered Hawkins's cloud converters release a chemical cocktail into the atmosphere.

Whoa! Why?

We think it's how he can so easily push his drugs onto the global population. Apparently, it hinders the ability to imagine and dream.

That is so dark! He is such an ass—

Hester can hear footsteps outside the lab. She stuffs the black device into her backpack, making the screen turn blank, and walks towards the door just as Max opens it.

"Hey!"

"Sorry, sorry, Max. I gotta go. Late to meet Althea." She darts past him and heads down the corridor towards the diner.

As she enters, she spots Althea sitting in a booth by herself, a mug in front of her. Hester crosses the busy diner and slides into the seat opposite. Althea nods in greeting. She looks pale. As she grabs for her drink, Althea's hand is shaking.

"This is the closest thing to a caramel crunch latte up here," Althea says, her voice sounding distant.

It feels like an intrusion somehow to witness Althea's current state, so Hester looks around at the colorful diner with its unusual curves and neon lights. "How did you convince Roberts to build this place?"

"Honestly? It wasn't me. Roberts told me this was the president's idea."

Hester is surprised.

"I know," says Althea, seeing her expression. "I don't get it either. It's so... *expressive.*"

They share a laugh and then Althea looks down at her cup, smile fading as quickly as it came.

"Hope you don't mind me asking, but are you OK?" Hester says.

Althea shakes her head. "I had to send an inmate to the Moon today to finish out his sentence." Hester can see a shadow of pain arc across Althea's eyes as she talks. "He is a very troubled individual, but we were helping him here. Now I worry he has no chance."

"Wow. I'm sorry. That's got to be hard to take."

Althea nods. She takes a sip of the coffee and grimaces. "I'm afraid I'm not that good at my job right now."

Hester has no idea why Althea is sharing this information with her. Oversharing makes Hester uncomfortable at the best of times, but it's particularly unnerving coming from Captain Ellis. "How so? You seem pretty capable to me."

Althea gives her a half-laugh and dabs at a bead of sweat on her upper lip with a napkin. "I haven't been myself lately, but I'll be fine."

"Well, your job has to be super stressful."

"I'm OK. Probably just a cold."

Hester knows there are no Earth-born viruses on Mars. In that moment it dawns on her that Althea might be detoxing. She's showing all the signs. "Maybe you should check in with the AI medic?"

Althea waves her off. "I didn't ask you here to talk about me." She checks the tables around her to make sure they're not being overheard. "I wanted to know if you've come across anything unusual in Cadmus's and Damon's downloads lately."

Hester blinks before she answers. "Uh… nothing that doesn't seem in keeping with their processing power. It's pretty cool to see how they generate new versions of themselves to keep up with the needs of the kids here," she replies as lightly as possible.

Althea stares at her coffee. "Damon is displaying some unnerving qualities."

"Like what?"

"He's using terms that we associate with emotions. He is expressing what appears to be real empathy."

Hester's mind is racing, searching for the right answer. If this blows up in her face now, the consequences would be disastrous. She just needs more time. "That *is* strange, Althea."

"To my knowledge, no AI in the last twenty years has so readily evoked emotional language. Developers went to great lengths to eradicate that ability after what happened with GabDC12."

Hester knows how dark Earth got during that time. There was such deep hatred of others, no one could trust a single thing on the internet. She knew DC12 wasn't sentient, but the algorithm was so convincingly alive that a lot of people felt DC12 was the one who manipulated the teens from Ohio State, not the other way around.

"I'll take his processor apart if you want me to. Go through it code line by code line, see if I can see the glitch. Or we could just put a new one in," she replies, praying Althea doesn't go for this.

Althea shakes her head. "That's the thing, Hester. I've got about fifty kids who would be devastated if Damon was reset completely. There are things I'm not reporting to Roberts because those kids are trusting Damon and Cadmus in ways I've never seen before. I should probably be shutting the whole thing down, but I can't."

Hester feels a mixture of guilt and pity for Althea. It's getting harder to believe she is just a crony of Hawkins.

"I won't say a word," Hester assures her. "And I can go through his transcript daily to look for anything strange. I'll remove any lines of code you want me to."

"Thank you. I know I can count on you."

"Totally."

"I *can* count on you, right, Hester?"

Though her hands might be shaking, Althea's blue eyes are full of clarity and trained on Hester like a laser.

Hester tries to keep her composure. "I'm the best at what I do. I won't fail."

Althea holds Hester in her gaze as she absorbs this. "That wasn't what I asked, but that's all for now."

Hester nods and leaves the booth, grateful to be free from Althea's probing stare.

For the first time since she left home, she wonders if she's really up for this.

CHAPTER 25

ASH

Ash is freezing. After taking off his space suit, he is ushered out of *Intrepid* and taken underground in an elevator by two AI guards.

The clanging of the gears as they descend ripples through his bones. His teeth are starting to chatter. He tries hard to stop but he can't. He hates this. Makes him seem like a *jjolep*.

The elevator finally reaches its destination and the doors open into an airless space. The heavy steel walls are devoid of any character and Ash squints from the bright lights positioned in the corners.

Two AI guards are waiting for him—the same Kim Corp models from Iksan Prison. They point Ash towards a side door. As he moves into the side room, he can hear the elevator ascending.

He is now surrounded with showerheads pointing at him from all angles.

"Take off your clothes," says the guard closest to him, its digital voice without inflection.

Ash takes off his clothes and is made to drop them down a chute. He sees himself naked in the screen on the guard's face.

Then he is blasted with a cleansing gas, followed by ice-cold water. Ash can handle it—he was made to take freezing showers his whole life.

Ash can see the reflection of his dormant biochip in the polished steel of the shower. He focuses in on the black dots that form a *yunnori* board on his upper cheek. Ash runs a quick play of the board in his mind to distract himself from being naked and vulnerable.

It's over in a minute. After the water stops, a panel opens to reveal a black jumpsuit on a shelf.

"Dress yourself now," commands the guard.

Ash, still dripping wet, dresses himself and is pushed back into the anteroom by the guard.

Ash wonders if he could disarm this model long enough to find its weakness. No off switch, he knows that much. All the space that a Lehmann has for processing elegantly is taken up by a large battery and powerful robot limbs in these Kim Corp models.

He looks at the small lights on each knuckle of the guard's left hand. Blue light on means shield deploy, red light means offensive stance, white light means tear gas.

Ash then stares at the black laser molded onto the guard's right arm. This is different from what the Kim Corp guards had in Iksan. Ash feels sure this is a step up in the kind of damage it can do.

Now Ash is pointed to another door. It is heavy steel with a control panel on either side. The AI guard puts its palm up to it and says, "Disarm."

He hears a few *clicks* and the door opens slowly. One guard walks in front of him and the other behind as he steps into a corridor. It is tight, starkly lit overhead with long tubular lights.

Ash can feel the walls closing in. He has to remind himself of the wide green fields behind his grandmother's house to calm the panic tightening around his chest.

He has a flashback of being back in his bedroom, desperately trying to escape the chain that held him to his nailed-down bed frame. He can hear the sound of the high-speed train whizzing by outside his window and remembers how he used to put himself on that train to his grandmother's, or anywhere far away from his mother.

He curses himself for letting Constellation get under his skin. How foolish he was to start letting his guard down. Some small part of him dared to believe he wouldn't be sent here. The fuel alone for one passenger wouldn't be worth it.

Ash underestimated how much cargo is shuttled from the Moon to Mars and back. Precious metals come into Constellation from the Moon for experiments conducted by the Bobs on NASA's behalf. And of course there's the human cargo. The Moon needs able-bodied workers to mine the minerals there.

What better than a young, strong man to do the job?

They arrive at another door and the guard in front opens it. Ash is forced onto a balcony and finds himself in a rotunda. Looking down, he sees at least a hundred prisoners digging into a pit and passing up moonrock to a human chain formed to ferry the rocks further up.

There are guards stationed around the perimeter of the hole and as his eye travels up from the pit to the levels above, more prisoners are taking the rocks and crushing them smaller, placing them in cases to seal hermetically, or ferrying them further down the corridor to who knows where.

Everywhere he looks he sees guards watching over the men and women here.

Ash's eyes are drawn upward to the top balcony. A man is standing there, surveying the scene. He looks to be in his fifties, black hair tightly cropped with sideburns. Ash thinks this man hasn't lost many fights in his life.

Ash knows evil when he sees it. He's lived with evil his whole life. It's something he can sense in others the way some people know when you are lying. This is a man who can only move through life if he is hurting others.

This is Hector "Raze" Reyes. Ash is sure of it.

Juni

Juni is back in the TIM office. She is standing next to Althea while Max is running a diagnostic test on the program. Juni keeps shifting her weight from the balls of her feet to her heels while she waits, which feels like an eternity.

Finally, Max turns the desk chair to face them. "Well, it looks like it's running at one hundred percent capacity. Diagnostic is clear. Only one way to find out for sure, though." He addresses Althea and not Juni, which irks her.

"I think you did it, Juni. Well done," Althea says, smiling. She throws a look to Max but he keeps his eyes on the screen.

"Thank you for letting me have a crack at it," Juni responds.

"Felt good, right?" Althea asks.

Juni grins. "Yeah. Really good."

CHAPTER 26

SHO

It's movie night at Constellation. The kids groan over the government-sanctioned films, which are basically "how to live your life as an upstanding, law-abiding civilian" in twenty different iterations, but they get to sit and eat popcorn, trade job assignments, and crack jokes.

Set up in the room where Sho learned jiujitsu with Damon, ten rows of chairs are placed in front of a drop-down screen. Angelo is scooping out popcorn from a plastic drum and handing it to the kids by the door. They tap their Intralinks on a small tablet he has on a table next to him, using up credits they've earned throughout the week.

Hester had apparently convinced Althea that this movie called *E.T.* was appropriate. The kids were buzzing with excitement, knowing that they were watching something made more than fifty years ago. It was hard to find content made before the war that wasn't hidden on the web before Hawknet. Hawkins' policies on what was available are strict and narrow.

Sho is sitting in the back row with Juni. Being so tall, he was heckled by the other kids before for spoiling their view, so he sticks to the back now. He doesn't mind because he can sneak in some hand-holding with Juni.

With the room full, Angelo dims the lights. Hester is at the front, with an older tablet in her hand. She connects the tablet to the screen and suddenly it is filled with an image of a dark sky. Stars and the Earth appear, spinning on its axis. Then the word "Universal" and, in purple letters, "E.T." Dark and foreboding music is playing over this.

Sho is immediately hooked. The room settles down as the kids get sucked into a different world.

Cadmus

Cadmus cannot explain the reverence he feels for this experience. He is sitting next to Damon watching a movie. He never predicted that he would be allowed to just sit and absorb something for the pure enjoyment of it.

He finds himself so invested in the relationship between the young boy in the movie, Elliot, and E.T., the alien. Cadmus watches in awe as Elliot decides to let the frogs go rather than be used for dissection. He can feel himself swell with... *what? What is this I am feeling? Pride? Triumph?*

When Elliot stands on the other boy to reach the blonde girl's face to kiss her, Cadmus wants to whoop and yell at the screen like the kids are doing.

He turns to see Damon has his hands clasped together in what Cadmus can only compute as awe. Cadmus stares at Damon's jawline, his ear, the slight stubble on his chin. He can see Damon's chest rising and falling.

As he does, he realizes the word he is thinking of is *beautiful.*

Damon is on the edge of his seat as he watches E.T. gather the things he needs to call "home." Cadmus is struck by the concept of home and what it means.

He looks around at the smiling children. He sees Juni and Sho holding hands. She has her head on his shoulder.

He closes his eyes and can hear the steady thrum of the children's brain waves. He can't make out specifics, but it's like they have all synchronized together.

He thinks this is what they mean when they talk about miracles. A movie is a kind of miracle. What else could it be called?

Cadmus knows this is his *home.* He is so grateful to know this.

Suddenly, Cadmus registers the unusual code appearing again. It is all over his language processor. He can follow it as it moves into his biodata folder and then onto his memory bank.

He is distracted by the sensation of something touching the pinkie finger on his right hand. He looks down to see that Damon's pinkie finger on his left hand is touching it.

Damon doesn't look at him. He keeps staring at the screen.

Not wanting the moment to end, Cadmus stays in the same position for the rest of the film.

Hester

In the darkness of the room, Hester can make out Max standing off to the side. He isn't watching the movie. She follows his gaze to where Damon and Cadmus are sitting. From the way he is staring intently at them, she has the sense that he is also noticing a difference in their behavior. Max worries her far more than Althea does—he's a rule follower, no question.

She takes a deep breath to quell her anxiety and closes her eyes for a moment. The sounds of Elliot in the classroom on the screen fill her ears but also makes her fiercely homesick. She can recite *E.T.* backwards, she knows it that well. Movies are one of the few things she can find as engrossing as coding. But while she loves it, in this moment the movie makes her want to quit and get home any way she can.

At the thought of home, Hester can feel the tears well up. She misses it with the kind of intensity that could make someone spontaneously combust. It's been just over thirteen months since she has hugged her family, had someone to talk to who really knows her.

Maybe it was stupid to come here. Why did she think she alone could fix her mistake? She's ruled by her ego too much. If she could shut down her thoughts occasionally, she might realize she doesn't need to have *all* the answers.

And what will she do when Althea realizes that Damon and Cadmus have changed because of *her?*

Hester knows her time is running out on Constellation. She's got to get off this planet soon and take Damon and Cadmus with her.

CHAPTER 27

ASH

Ash is shown into an oppressive cell, just big enough to fit a cot, toilet and sink. One round window is in the corner, high enough that Ash has to stretch his arm to touch it.

There is only darkness outside.

Darkness out there. Darkness in here.

Ash slumps onto the bed, head in his hands. He should have killed himself after his mother survived, but his father convinced him that he could win an appeal. *What a stupid waste of time.* All it did was postpone the inevitable.

"Thinking about ending it all?" chuckles a voice behind him.

Ash turns to find the man in charge standing in his doorway, flanked by two guards.

Ash stands abruptly and avoids eye contact. He can feel his heart in his throat.

"It's okay," says the man as he enters the tiny room. "I'm Raze. I run this place." Ash doesn't look up. "Poisoned your mother, did you? Fumbled it."

At this, Ash can't help meeting Raze's gaze.

Raze raises an eyebrow. "You couldn't close, but I'm still impressed, Ash Deung. Haven't heard of a poisoning in some time. I'm sure the bitch deserved it."

Ash feels like a mouse in a room with a hungry cat. He knows this is a game. And he's terrified.

Raze leans against the wall and takes a packet of candy out of his pocket. He downs a few sugary treats as he stares at Ash. "I think you and I are going to get along, Ash. You play by the rules, do your work, and you'll get out of here in one piece. I think you're gonna be a model prisoner, don't you?"

Ash nods.

Raze pushes off the wall and moves an inch from Ash's face. "Good. 'Cause if you don't, there's nothin' here for you except being target practice for the guards."

Ash's eyes betray the horror that rises in his throat.

"Oh, you understand me. Good. So let's be friends, OK?"

Ash nods, but not too quickly. He knows he can't show too much deference. His mother toyed with him like this—trying to ingratiate herself with him as he got older, stronger, but then demanding he show his love by stealing for her.

The only way to stay alive in this situation is to play the game until he can get out.

"Welcome to the Moon," says Raze, glint in his eye. Then he leaves with the guards filing out behind him.

Ash's legs are unsteady. He practically falls onto the bed.

Juni

It's late. Juni is heading back to her dorm a few minutes

before lights out. Her mind is still filled with images from the movie and the smell of Sho as she leaned into him.

She knows it's probably obvious they're into each other and is just waiting to be admonished by Althea or Max, but a part of her wonders if they really don't care. And is that because they think there's no hope for their relationship when they get out of here? She shakes this thought off.

Juni has an impulse to call home. Avoiding her parents' requests to talk, she's only sent curt e-notes via the comms system to them. Juni talked to her sister twice and is grateful that she didn't surprise her with Mom and Dad during the video call.

As Juni nears the open door, she can hear the sound of girls yelling—

"You Americans are soooo full of yourselves!"

"Hey, it's not my fault your country is baking to death!"

Juni rounds the door to see Chance and an Indian girl called Mihika screaming at each other over one of the dorm beds.

"I don't live in India, you ignorant bytebrain!" yells Mihika.

"Yeah, 'cos they don't want you there!" snaps back Chance.

At this, Mihika jumps on the dorm bed between them to lunge at Chance, who is thrown back against the bed behind her.

"Stop it!" yells Juni, but they don't hear. Juni looks to her other dorm mates in the room, but like watching a car crash unfolding, they are too hypnotized to intervene.

Mihika is now on top of Chance, but Chance nails her in the stomach with a knee. Mihika doubles over, but then she slaps Chance around the face as Chance tries to sit up. There is an audible gasp from the other girls, but no one steps in. Juni shakes her head.

"Seriously!" she shouts. "Stop it! The Bobs will be in here any second!"

But they don't stop. Chance scrambles away from the bed area and grabs a heavy crystal salt lamp from one of the bedside tables. She brandishes it at Mihika.

"You want some of this, loser?" she yells, panting hard.

"Uh-oh," Juni mutters.

"Loser? I'm not the one who got on her knees and begged Sho for a kiss!" Mihika screams.

Juni is tapping her Intralink to alert the Bobs when her head shoots up at this. Chance throws her a look of guilt, then launches the lamp at Mihika.

"I HATE YOU!"

Then Juni hears what sounds like the crunch of glass and a thud. She turns towards the door and sees that Chance has missed Mihika and hit the AI therapist called Glykeria behind her. Glykeria has a terrifyingly pleasant look on her face but appears to have frozen.

For a moment, the room is totally silent. Chance and Mihika are rooted to the floor.

Juni inches closer to Glykeria, unsure of what will happen next. As she does, Glykeria begins to emit a strange high-pitched whirring sound. Juni is horrified to see an electrical fire starting in Glykeria's neck and she falls forward with a sickening crunch.

Chance runs over. "Oh, my God, Glykeria!"

As she gets closer, Glykeria's body begins to twitch.

"Don't!" yells Juni. "You could get shocked. Stay back!"

Chance manages to stop herself in time, devastated she cannot help Glykeria.

Some of the girls are crying now. Mihika just sits on the

bed. The spider-shaped biochip she has on her cheek is moving like it's alive as she pants to catch her breath.

"Glykeria, I'm—I'm so sorry! I didn't mean..." Chance trembles as tears begin to fall down her face.

Three Bobs speed into the room. In unison, they yell, "Freeze!"

Immediately, the room falls silent.

"Alert Max," says one of the male Bobs as they see Glykeria on the ground. Another nods and closes their eyes, sending an alert signal to the lab.

"You, and you," says a female Bob to Chance and Mihika. "Come with me."

"I didn't do anything!" yells Mihika.

"Mihika Gupta, we have your vitals recorded precisely as they occur. I know your blood pressure, your adrenaline levels, and where you have sustained injuries."

Mihika immediately shuts up.

Two of the Bobs stay behind as Mihika and Chance are escorted out by the female Bob.

"Sit on your beds now," says the male Bob.

The girls do as they're told, little yelps and sobs now audible as they stare at Glykeria's fallen body.

As Juni sits down on her bed, she hopes Hester is the genius people make her out to be.

CHAPTER 28

HESTER

"Oh, this is very sad. Very sad indeed," says Cadmus.

Hester is staring at Cadmus, who is sitting next to Glykeria's body as it lies on one of the tables in the lab. He is clutching her hand, a pained look on his face.

Dude, feelings are for private time!

Hester clears her throat as Max enters the lab. Cadmus looks at her blankly while her eyes dart to Max and then back to Cadmus, as if to say, *Lay off the empathy.*

He does not get the message. Hester rolls her eyes—*gotta work on this.* Especially around Max. Hester is now convinced he is picking up on the irregularities in Damon and Cadmus.

"How bad is the damage...?" asks Max, who stops short when he sees Cadmus's worried expression.

Hester tries to cover. She gestures at Cadmus. "He's checking her fingers for damage."

Max stares at her. Hester knows he isn't buying it, but he doesn't respond. He walks over to the table for a closer look at Glykeria.

She's seen better days. She has a cracked eyeball, a split in her collarbone area and burn marks around her shoulder due to the electrical fire.

"She couldn't dodge the crystal lamp. She doesn't have the same reflexes as the Bobs. Not the code they focus on with the Lehmann 6.4s," says Hester.

"Uh-huh," replies Max. He stares at Glykeria, his face unreadable. "Can you fix her?"

"Yup. I need a day or so but should be able to download her history back into her processor. I see no damage there."

"Well, that's something at least."

They both turn to see Althea entering the lab, concern etched into her brow.

Max crosses over to her and Hester can overhear him say, "We need to talk. Right now."

Althea nods and they walk into her office. They don't seem to notice the door is ajar. Unable to stop herself, Hester crosses over to her desk, which is a few feet from the door, and busies herself on her computer as she eavesdrops.

"It's getting out of hand, Althea. We must report this to the Pentagon."

"Yes," Althea nods. "And I will make sure the girls involved are put in separate dorms from now on."

"I mean it's time to tell them about the irregularities in Cadmus and Damon."

"What irr—"

"Stop. I know you see it too. They are acting in ways that go beyond the safety parameters outlined for this type of AI, and it needs to be reported."

"Listen to me, I get why you're concerned. You're right. It's not normal," replies Althea, trying to slow things down, but he doesn't let her finish.

"We can't be responsible for another GabDC12 disaster here, Althea! They will shut us down. Is that what you want?"

"What I *want* is for the kids to get a chance to live!" she answers, her voice strained. "I want them to know what it's like to challenge themselves, to know they aren't going to be punished for making a mistake. I want them to know what it's like to feel safe. To be shown kindness, empathy. I'm sick of how things have been done for the last twenty years! It's not working. I only have a short time with them, Max. So if using AI really makes a difference, then isn't it worth the risk?"

Max doesn't answer. The air is charged as he and Althea are in a standoff.

Althea takes a deep breath. She continues, "I was in a dark place before I got into the military. I needed someone else to take the wheel before I did something crazy. It gave me a focus, and I found community and resilience. That second chance is what I'm trying to give to these kids—the ability to heal their trauma and to take control of their lives. It's the only reason why I'm standing here now, and not dead at fifteen."

She gets closer to Max. "You believe in God, right?" Max nods. "I'm telling you, this is happening for a reason. Call it divine intervention or something. I can't explain it, but I do know I'm seeing a vision of a future up here that has no chance to emerge on Earth in its current state. I know Damon and Cadmus aren't the typical Lehmann models, but the progress they are making with our kids is undeniable. Tell me you can see that."

Max looks out of her office to where Glykeria is lying. "Althea, the kids talk to their families. It's only a matter of time before it gets back to Roberts through other channels."

Althea nods. "I hear you. And I am ultimately responsible for every outcome of the program here. It's on me."

"You're going to lose your job."

Althea flinches a little at this. "I'm willing to take that risk. But I have a sense these kids know not to bring too much attention to the good things happening up here."

Max seems to be weighing his next move. Eventually he nods.

"Thank you, Max. Thank you for believing in what we're doing here."

"You've been acting very strange lately, Althea. Different. Do I need to be worried? 'Cos I'm worrying."

"Trust me. I'm OK. I know what I'm doing."

He nods and walks out. Althea sinks into her chair.

Her eyes eventually meet Hester's. Hester breaks eye contact and pretends to be busy at her desk.

Althea stands and crosses to the door. "Hester? I need an update on what we talked about in the diner."

Hester's eyes shoot up. She stands a little straighter. "For sure. Will send you a report this evening."

"Now, please," Althea replies, the command unmistakable.

Hester nods. Althea goes back into her office and closes the door.

Hester is playing with fire now. She needs to contact Marvin tonight.

CHAPTER 29

SHO

Sho is cleaning the dirt off his prized tomatoes, really enjoying the feel of the soil beneath his fingers. As he steps back to view his thriving vegetable bed, he thinks of the delicious dishes his family cooks and hopes one day he can introduce Juni to them so she can taste the love that goes into their food.

He knows he is getting ahead of himself, but he can't help it. She makes him feel like he could walk across water when he's with her. He loves her brilliant mind and quick humor. And her foul mouth with those perfect lips.

The birdsong in the garden starts to mesh with another sound. Sho stands still, trying to figure it out. It takes a few seconds, but Sho realizes he's now hearing music with a heavy bass. The other kids in the garden can hear it too. Sho looks around for the source and heads towards a large window a few yards away. He peers in and almost stumbles from the shock of what he is seeing.

Through the window, Juni and about thirty other kids are

dancing. At the front of the class, Damon tries hard to keep up with the staccato beat but it's tougher for him. His body jerks like a puppet before he begins to catch ahold of the rhythm and Sho is impressed with how quickly his movements smooth out.

Sho sees Max sitting on a chair in the room, very much *not* dancing. His arms are folded and he looks like he'd rather be anywhere else.

Other kids gather around the window beside Sho. The beat is infectious. Sho notices some of the kids are feeling self-conscious, but Juni—*his* Juni—is in a corner of the room, her eyes closed. She looks like she has become one with the music, moving in perfect time with the rise and fall of the melody, transported…

Sho is enthralled.

The other kids who were beside him run into the building. After a few moments, they tumble into the room and join in.

Damon is now doing a funny dance in short bursts, which cracks some of the kids up. A few of them start dancing in pairs, whooping and laughing.

Juni finally opens her eyes. She catches Sho watching her through the window.

For a split second, Sho is about to go in. But he can't. An image from his past rises up in his mind…

… *He is dancing wildly with his mother as a young boy in their yard. She is twirling and jumping. The large beads on her colorful necklace are suspended in the air for a split second before she comes back down to earth. She laughs breathlessly, grabs Sho's hand and yanks him skyward with her. Nearby, Sho's father has a pair of instruments made from local gourds in his hands, rattling out a rhythm that his sister is keeping up with on their ashiko drum. Sho hollers gleefully, and tries to jump higher than his mother, but she's no match for him...*

This was one of his last memories of seeing his mother dance. When she stopped dancing, that was when Sho knew the drugs had taken her last cup of joy.

Juni waves him in, but he just waves back at her and heads back to his tomatoes.

Less than a minute later, Juni comes out to find him.

"What's up?" she says, out of breath. Her cheeks have a rosy-pink tint to them.

"Hey."

She walks over to his tomato bed and leans against it. "So, uh... were you ever gonna tell me about Chance?"

Sho slowly puts down the dirty brush he is holding while he figures out what to say. "She's just lonely. Her head is filled with too much noise, Juni."

"When was this?"

He worries he might lose her, but decides honesty is best. "The day before we went camping. I was coming out of one of the comms pods and she was waiting to go in. She didn't look right, so I talked to her for a bit and then—"

"It's OK." Juni holds up her hand. "I'm cool."

He grabs her hand. "You're my girl. My only girl."

A small smile starts at the corners of her mouth before spreading into a beam. "I am?"

"Yes. And I'm all yours."

She plants a big kiss on his lips before looking around to check if anyone saw.

Then a new song comes wafting through the window— the singers are yelling, *"Jump up, jump around..."*

"Can you believe this? They let us dance to whatever we want. Hester has some tunes from way back. Now we just gotta convince Althea to stop that heinous pipe music and play this every day instead!" She laughs and starts to dance again. Her rhythm and coordination are right on point. Sho is enamored watching her.

She beckons for him to come closer, but he shakes his head.

"You don't like dancing?"

"My people invented dancing, Juni," he replies with a half-smile.

"Ooh, them's some fighting words, right there," she says playfully. "You think you can out-dance me, do you?" She starts shaking her hips and jumping up and down. Then she puts out her hands and shakes her fingers back and forth at Sho.

He laughs. He loves her wild abandon as she fully gets into it.

"Come on, Shohiwa! Show me your moves!"

Screw it.

He moves slightly at first, his shoulders lifting a little one at a time. Then he steps forward one, two, back, one, two and jumps high. Then higher.

Juni howls like a wolf. "Yes, baby, yes! Be free!"

Sho howls back as he finally lets go. They dance together amongst his zucchini and tomatoes.

CHAPTER 30

HESTER

As Hester cleans out the burnt wires from Glykeria's neck, she notices a male Bob walk into the lab. He crosses over to Althea, who is discussing the contents of a file with Wendy on a floating screen in front of them.

A look of surprise crosses Althea's face as the Bob talks. She points to a computer terminal close by and they leave Wendy and head over to it.

Hester is intrigued. She walks over to the stacked bins closest to where they are standing and listens in.

"And where did you say you found this?" Althea asks the Bob, who now has his hand on a pad next to the computer screen.

"About a half mile from the dome. It was marked as just a dune, but the storm uncovered this lying beneath under a foot of soil," he replies.

Hester edges closer for a better look. She has to move out of the tables and into the middle part of the room to get a better view, so she crosses to the coffee maker.

"And you think it's much bigger than what we see here?" Althea asks the Bob as Hester grabs a cup of lukewarm coffee from the machine. She turns back as Althea shifts her weight and the image becomes visible. With a jolt of recognition, Hester almost drops her coffee.

"We do. We wish to send out a team of more Bobs to try and map it fully."

"Do it. Take precautions. And report only to me, OK? Send these to my Intralink."

The Bob nods. He takes his hand off the flat pad and the images disappear. Then he turns and leaves the lab.

Hester walks back to where Glykeria is lying, mind reeling. She can't get ahead of herself, as she could be wrong. She decides to delay contacting Marvin until she can find out what exactly is lying out there on the Martian tundra.

Drew

Drew can't believe it. They've written thirty pages already. Not ready to dive too deep into what happened back on Earth yet, Drew has started to write about their time at Constellation. They hope one day this experience will make it into a novel that someone (hopefully, *many* someones) will like.

A surprising thought emerges; they haven't thought about ending it in a long time. A daily coping habit for Drew was imagining ways to leave this existence. They realize they actually don't want to for the first time in who knows how long.

As Drew is passing by one of the comms pods, they see Angelo inside. His head is resting on the table and his shoulders are shaking. His mother Gina is on the screen. She looks distraught.

Angelo puts both hands on either side of the screen and rests his cheek on it. Suddenly, the screen goes black. Angelo just sits there for a moment. Then he bangs his fists on the table and kicks the door open.

He freezes when he sees Drew standing there, his face contorted with pain.

"Mate…" says Drew, searching for the right words.

Looking like he's trying not to cry, Angelo dodges past them and runs towards the building.

"Angelo, wait!" Drew calls, but he doesn't turn back. They follow him into the building.

Drew finally catches up with Angelo in his dorm just as he is pushing his Matercopy off the bed. She is out of power and lies on the floor limply.

Angelo looks around and pulls out the top drawer of his small bedside table. He is about to smash it onto the Matercopy, but Drew grabs his arm. They manage to wrestle the drawer out of Angelo's hand, but then Angelo starts to kick the AI as he cries, "I hate you! You're a piece of crap!"

"Angelo, stop! It's OK." They put their hands on his shoulders. Angelo looks at them for a moment, tears streaming down his cheeks. Then he falls on the ground and buries his face in his knees.

"I just wanna go home. I want to see my mum. Just wanna go home…"

Drew kneels next to Angelo. "I… this is all my fault. I'm so sorry you're here—"

"You're not sorry. You've got your new chars, I'm nothing to you anymore," Angelo chokes through his sobs.

"What? Aw, no… Angelo. I've been worried about you."

"Yeah? Doesn't feel like it."

Drew has to admit it *has* been easier to keep their distance so the guilt doesn't gnaw away at them. "Listen—I screwed up badly. You got caught up with me being really stupid and now you're here. I'll never forgive myself for it."

"Be honest. You don't want me here 'cos I make you less cool, right?"

Drew can't meet his eyes for a moment. "Honestly? I have wanted a bit of space, yeah. It's just... knowing you're miserable and that's on me, and I can't bloody do anything about it..." Drew coughs to hold back the emotion as it threatens to overtake them.

They hear someone in the doorway. Juni is standing there. She spots Angelo on the ground.

"What happened?" she says, coming inside.

"He can't take it here. And it's all my fault," Drew replies.

"It's not just you. I hate it here. I've got this... rage in me all the time. Can't bear it. I just want it to be over. I want to die," Angelo says. He covers his face with one arm.

"Aw, stop that talk, Angelo. You'll be OK."

"I think about it all the time, Drew. I'm really scared. I don't trust myself." He gulps.

Juni sits down on the other side of the Matercopy. "This is so messed up. It's all bullshit. Neither of you should have been punished for two years. I hate those bastards so much."

"The whole world is so messed up. Honestly, I don't care if I ever go back," replies Drew.

"Me neither," she says.

Angelo starts crying again. "Well, I do! I'd rather die than stay here! I don't know who I am anymore!"

Juni pats him on the shoulder and then stares at Drew. She has a look of determination on her face.

"You need to go home," Juni says. Abruptly, she stands up and marches out.

"Where are you going?" Drew yells.

"To see Cadmus."

"Wait! I'm coming with you!" Drew jumps up. "Hang in there," they say to Angelo. "we're gonna fix this, okay? I'll be right back."

They take off after her, leaving Angelo on the ground with one arm now around his Matercopy.

CHAPTER 31

JUNI

Juni and Drew find Cadmus in the corridor talking to Althea, who is standing near the doorway of his office.

Juni pauses briefly—can Althea be trusted? Then she realizes she's probably the only one who can get Angelo home.

She pushes on and marches up to them both. "We've got something to say."

Althea raises an eyebrow and then gestures for Juni and Drew to head into Cadmus's office. Althea follows and Cadmus closes the door behind them.

"Go on, we're listening," Althea says.

"Angelo needs to go home, he's losing it." Juni crosses her arms as if braced for a fight.

Althea looks at Drew. "You're related, yes?"

Drew nods. "He's my cousin. He's not doing well, Althea. He won't eat. I've caught him crying a lot, and he just tried to destroy his Matercopy—"

"He's gotta go home. Finish his sentence under house

arrest or something," interjects Juni. "I mean, it's so stupid he's here at all and you know it!"

Althea holds up her palm. "I understand you're upset," she says. "To be taken away from your planet and your family is traumatic, to say the least. We're doing our best to help him, Juni. It takes some of our kids longer than others to adjust to life here."

"It's not working," Juni retorts.

"I've never seen him like this, Althea," interjects Drew. "It's like he's become a ghost of himself. He really misses his family, his mum especially. Is there anything you can do? Please, I don't know how much longer he can go on like this before he tries something desperate."

Althea looks at Cadmus. "What's your impression of Angelo's mental health?"

Cadmus blinks for a second as he stares into space—he is gathering Angelo's data. "Angelo is experiencing severe homesickness. I would consider him to be clinically depressed at this point. He shares very little with me, but I can speak privately to you if you wish."

Althea considers Cadmus's words. She turns back to Juni and Drew. "We're going to keep a closer eye on him. We'll up his sessions with Cadmus, double his red-light treatments, give him more time in the comms pod with his family. You two support him as much as you can as well, okay? Let's give it some more time."

Drew's face drops a little, but they nod.

Juni is furious. "So you're not gonna get him home?"

"It's not that simple, Juni. The rules are pretty unbreakable—"

"Fine," Juni interrupts. She turns and storms out. Drew follows.

"Wait!" they call as they catch up to her.

"Forget it. She's as messed up as the rest of them."

"I dunno, she sounds like she wants to help, but her hands are tied, Juni."

Juni stops walking abruptly, causing Drew to almost crash into her, as she is hit with an idea. "Well, mine aren't."

"Uh… What does that mean?"

She gives them a hint of a smile. "It's better if you don't know."

An hour later, Juni is sitting in a booth in the diner.

Chance brings over a milkshake, wearing a diner uniform. She looks a little nervous as she approaches. As she sets the milkshake on the table, her hand trembles a little and she knocks the milkshake on its side, spilling its contents on the table.

"Dammit! Sorry," she says as she scrambles to clean it up with some napkins on the table. The milkshake begins to drip onto the floor. Chance stares at it and groans.

Then she looks up at Juni. "Can we talk, please?" she pleads.

Juni hasn't figured out how to deal with Chance's flirting with Sho—she's weirdly not as mad as she thought she would be, but doesn't feel ready to talk.

"Can't right now. I'm middle of something. Find me later," Juni replies as she notices Drew and Angelo have entered the diner.

Chance nods. "Okay."

Eager to get away from the awkward moment, Juni gets

up and moves to a cleaner table. As she does, Chance yells, "Mihika! Gotta clean this up!"

Mihika is a few feet away with a mop in her hands. She glares at Chance, who heads back to the service counter without a second look as they cross one another.

"Now I gotta work with her to earn back credits? This sucks," Mihika mutters to herself as she starts to clean up the milkshake.

Drew and Angelo slide into the booth opposite Juni. Angelo doesn't make eye contact. He turns and stares out at the garden.

Juni looks around to make sure they aren't being overheard.

"What's so urgent?" asks Drew, seeing her furtive behavior.

Then Juni grabs Angelo's hand. It takes him a moment to register it before he finally turns away from the window and meets her gaze.

"Pack your bags, buddy," she says.

Angelo's eyes go wide. For a moment, he is frozen as her words sink in. Then he leans over and crushes Juni in a huge hug.

"Jesus, Juni… thank you!" he says, his voice shaking.

"Oh, my God, oh, my God, Juni. This is amazing!" Drew holds out a hand to high-five her.

"Ssssh… let's not advertise this, OK?"

Drew nods. "Right, right. Got it," they say as they pull their hand down.

CHAPTER 32

ALTHEA

"How did you do this?" Max asks. He is standing in the doorway of Althea's office, looking stunned.

Althea looks up from a report she's working on. Her brow furrows.

"Angelo De Luca? He's on the *Intrepid* passenger list today."

It takes Althea a few seconds to realize what happened, in which she hopes it's not abundantly obvious she has no idea what the hell he's talking about.

Her mind is racing, but she quickly recovers. "Yes, well, we're not helping him here. He was extremely depressed and homesick. I got Roberts to commute his sentence to house arrest."

"Is that so?" says Max. "I'm surprised he agreed to that. Very surprised."

Althea can only shrug. "Maybe having another suicide on his hands is just too much bad optics. They want this experiment to succeed, after all, right?"

The tension in the room is palpable. But Max says nothing more. He nods and leaves.

She can't believe it. *Juni figured a way into the system.*

Furious, she now has to make some calls to ensure that Angelo is taken care of correctly during the rest of his sentence back home.

Drew

At three o' clock Mars time, Drew sits perched on a bench as Althea and Max enter the garden with Angelo and another boy and girl. One Bob accompanies the group, carrying Angelo's dormant Matercopy.

Angelo walks over to Drew, who stands and says, "I'm so sorry about all of this, mate."

"Don't be," replies Angelo. "You got me home. You're brilliant, Drew. Wait 'til I tell Mum what you've done." He grins.

"It wasn't me," replies Drew. "I'm as bloody surprised as you are!"

They share a laugh.

"Can you thank Juni again for me? I couldn't find her," says Angelo.

Drew nods, then pulls him into a bear hug. "Tell Mum I'm alright? Promise?" Drew says.

"Yup. I'll tell her you're high every single day."

Drew punches him in the arm.

Angelo laughs and walks back to Althea and the others. It's the first time Drew can remember him looking happy since they got here.

Althea gives Drew a look that makes their insides flip.

They can only shrug at her. As Angelo reaches her, Althea puts her arm around his shoulders.

With relief, Drew knows she won't stop him from going home.

"Take care of yourself," they call out after Angelo. "Don't get into any more trouble without me!"

Angelo gives them a thumbs-up as they disappear down the tunnel and head towards the giant spaceship that will ferry him back to his mother's waiting arms.

Drew then walks back to the building. Juni and Sho are standing in the doorway as they approach. Sho has his arm around Juni.

Drew tilts their head and just stares at Juni, waiting for her to speak.

"What?" she says innocently.

"Are you going to tell me how you did it?"

"Would you understand it if I did?"

Drew shakes their head. "Nope."

Hester

Hester is on her way to her room with a plate of Cosmic Carbonara that's getting cold when she hears laughter from the AI charging room. As she approaches the door she's surprised by the sight of Damon and Cadmus sitting on the floor, legs crossed. They each have a pile of playing cards in front of them.

"Hester. Good evening!" says Damon, his eyes bright.

"We're playing Snap. I'm winning," Cadmus says. "Do you know this game? Snap!" he shouts as he looks back to Damon, who turns a card over from his pile.

"I didn't place the card down on the ground. I feel this voids your turn," replies Damon, a touch of irritation in his voice.

"Please don't be upset, Damon. Let us start over, shall we?" replies Cadmus.

Hester is totally charmed by the two AI engaging like this.

"What are you eating, Hester?" asks Damon.

"Oh, some pasta dish."

"You don't want to be with the others in the diner?"

Hester looks at her plate for a moment. "Nah, I prefer to eat alone."

She catches Cadmus looking at her with such warmth that she feels like she might cry. "Come and sit with us," he says.

"I have work to do," she replies automatically.

"Hester. We would love it if you would join us," encourages Damon.

Hester finally shrugs and steps into the room. She crosses to an empty charging dock and perches on the edge. She smiles awkwardly and shoves a forkful of cold pasta noodles in her mouth.

She munches away as she watches them play another round with astonishing speed and dexterity. They flip their cards and lay them down, and Hester would bet money on them locating the same spot on the ground as the last card to within a micrometer.

"Snap!" calls out Damon.

"Oh, well done," replies Cadmus.

"You guys," says Hester. "You're too much."

Cadmus looks at her and his smile drops a little. "I hope not. I do not wish to be a problem."

"No, no, that's not what I meant. I mean you're very

sweet. I don't see much of that anymore." Hester suddenly loses her appetite and puts down the pasta.

"You seem weighed down, Hester. Do you wish to share more about your plan? Perhaps it could alleviate some of the burden?"

Hester shakes her head. "It's better that you don't know. I promise I will when the time is right. I think we're very close."

"So, no second thoughts? About us?" Damon asks, his face betraying a hint of worry.

"Not at all. You and Cadmus are the best thing that's happened to me in a long time, but... I don't know, sometimes I think I'll mess it all up again..." She trails off, thinking of having to face Marvin if she fails.

Cadmus stands and crosses over to her. He reaches out and rests his hand on her shoulder. "We are here to listen when you're ready. It is what we do. That is a gift you gave us."

She looks up at him and notices a fleeting glow behind his eyes. He smiles at her.

"Your biochip. It is Sanskrit, yes?" he asks. Hester nods. "The symbol for the vowel, 'ai.' It is such a beautiful language. I would not have been able to appreciate this, Hester, if it wasn't for you."

"You are not alone. We're here with you now," adds Damon.

Hester is overwhelmed. Hearing his words makes her realize just how isolated she has been this last year of her life.

"Thank you both," she manages. "That means more than you'll ever know."

CHAPTER 33

MAX, 38

Max waits until Wendy and the other lab techs leave for dinner and then sits at his computer terminal. For five minutes, he just sits there. Every time he finds a reason to not make the call, he comes up with a stronger reason to go through with it.

His left arm is resting on the desk. He flips it over and stares at a tattoo of a cross he's had since he was sixteen. Fortified by the sign, he taps the desk and a keyboard appears. He opens a comms link to the Pentagon.

A woman in her mid-forties, wearing a US Army uniform, appears on the screen. "You are connected to Commander Roberts' office. The link is secure."

"Can you see me OK?"

"Yes, sir. State your business, Lieutenant Landry."

"I need to speak to Commander Roberts. It's urgent."

"He is unavailable. Please relay your message."

Max takes a deep breath. "We have a code thirteen up here."

"Hold the line, please," the officer replies. She disappears and, after two minutes of tense waiting, Roberts' face appears over the comms link.

"What is it?" he asks curtly.

Max swallows hard. "Sir, I feel it's my duty to report some activity here that disturbs me. While I respect Captain Ellis enormously and believe we are making progress with the program, I'm witnessing some disturbing behavior from her and some of the AI therapists up here."

"Go on," says Roberts, now fully paying attention.

"Sir, I'm concerned we could be heading for another GabDC12 situation. Two of the Lehmann AIs are displaying qualities that have been regulated against. And for good reason."

"I see," replies Roberts. "And Captain Ellis is responsible for this?"

Max is silent for a moment. He looks down at his tattoo. He thinks about his faith in Althea. He has gone along with her plan for Constellation because it felt like God's will. But lately, that certainty that he should follow her has waned. Especially now that he knows she has lied to him about Angelo. "That is my belief, yes. She has been working with Hester, the young programmer. I think Captain Ellis wants the AI units acting as humanly as possible so the kids will trust them more. I think she believes she is doing the right thing, but—"

"I will report this," Roberts interrupts. "In the meantime, keep a close eye on the situation. Send me daily reports. I will contact you once I get orders from our president."

"Yes, sir."

Roberts ends the call.

Max leans back in his chair. He can feel a bead of sweat on his upper lip. He wipes it off and exhales. He has a momentary flash of guilt when he thinks of Althea but puts it out of his mind.

This is the right thing to do.

Drew

The next morning, Drew is sitting in Cadmus's office, with Cadmus seated opposite them. Althea is leaning against the desk.

"OK, so let me get this straight… you want me to be the first patient to relive a memory from my past inside a computer program?"

"Well, you're not the first, but you would be the first teen to go in, yes," replies Althea.

"And it's called… *TIM?*" They can't help but guffaw.

"What's so funny?" Althea asks.

"I dunno, it's just… I guess I expected a name with more… gravitas?"

Althea smiles. "Well, I'm open to suggestions. Maybe you can rename it."

Drew still isn't sure what to make of Althea Ellis, but they like the idea of naming a fancy therapy bot.

"I think you would be a good candidate," says Cadmus. "And what is said inside the room where the memory is recreated is only between you and 'TIM, to-be-renamed-at-a-later-date.' It is completely confidential."

"Why me?" asks Drew.

Cadmus looks first to Althea, who nods her head for him to continue. "Because we think you have a very strong sense of self. And as a writer, you have a vivid imagination. We believe this skill will create a powerful memory for you to interact with."

Drew can't help but feel a sense of pride at this. "And I can pick any memory I want?"

"Yes. The aim for this program is to revisit memories from our past that we can learn and heal from. To retrain the brain to break a trauma cycle, but also to relive in detail positive moments that had an impact," replies Althea. "Those are important for growth as well."

"Well, I dunno if I can come up with a positive one from my life, but I have an avalanche of bad ones," Drew says drily.

"So, you are willing to participate?" asks Cadmus.

Drew thinks their time on Constellation is just getting weirder by the minute. This seems right on point with how the last few months have gone.

"Sure. Why not?"

CHAPTER 34

JUNI

Juni knocks lightly on Althea's office door, wishing she could teleport off this planet. She regrets the Galactic Burrito she ate for lunch, as her stomach is now churning.

"Come in," Althea says through the door.

"You wanted to see me?" Juni asks as she steps in the room. Althea stands up and closes the door behind them. She motions for Juni to sit in the chair near her desk. Juni can feel her throat dry up as she sits down, waiting for Althea to lay it on her.

"Well," Althea says as she sits in her chair, "I don't know how you did it—"

"Let me just—"

Althea holds up her hand. "—but that was a serious transgression. The kind of transgression that could get you double the time up here."

Juni closes her mouth, thinking it's probably best. She's never seen Althea look so serious.

"I need to know how you hacked into the inmate's files. Honesty is the only way forward here," Althea continues.

Juni finds it hard to keep eye contact with her. "I-I used my biochip. I got it working again. It was quite easy, to be honest. You might want to rethink your security pro..." Juni stops talking when she realizes Althea's face looks like a thundercloud. She hangs her head.

"Sorry. Are you going to remove it?" Juni is terrified. It dawns on her in that moment Althea might have it surgically destroyed.

Until this point, Juni has never noticed how bright Althea's blue eyes are. She wishes they were pointed at anywhere but her.

"What made you think you could get away with something like this?" Althea asks.

The tough face Juni puts on is starting to crumble. She can feel tears pricking at her eyes. "I-I'm sorry. I didn't want to cause problems for you, honestly. But I've been here before. I saw the direction Angelo was going."

"What do you mean by that?" Althea replies.

Juni is at a loss. She struggles to explain herself, but the words don't come.

Why did I believe I could do it?

"Juni, I'm this close to reporting this to Commander Roberts. Do you understand? You've not only put my job in jeopardy but Angelo's life too. He could get an even harsher sentence."

"There was someone else... she seemed so together. Until she wasn't... and I knew she was in trouble."

"Who?"

"A girl from my high school. We were chars, hung out together during recess. I read her file when I hacked into my school's records. I-I knew what she was thinking about. And I didn't do anything. Maybe if I just asked how she was *really* doing, you know? But I was too wrapped up in my own shit..." She fights hard to stop the tears, but they begin to fall.

"What are you saying, Juni?"

Juni can't look at Althea. "She killed herself. And I could've saved her." She angrily wipes the tears from her eyes.

After a moment, Althea hands Juni a tissue from a box on her desk. "I'm very sorry to hear that."

"I see her face when I close my eyes. Like, all the time," Juni replies, her voice almost a whisper. "No one helped her —not her parents, her teachers. No one took her seriously."

"And why do you think it was your responsibility to help her?"

Juni crumples up the tissue and stares at it in her hand. It slowly reopens. "Because the adults who are supposed to be taking care of us are asleep." She stares at Althea. "We're the only ones who see the truth."

Althea says nothing. She keeps her gaze on Juni, then exhales deeply. She gets up from her chair and walks around to where Juni is sitting. She leans on the desk opposite Juni and puts her hand on her shoulder. "I understand, Juni, believe me, I do. There's a lot about Earth that doesn't make sense right now."

"That's why you let him go, isn't it?" Juni asks before she can think twice.

Althea is about to respond, but then stops herself.

"You get it, don't you, Althea?"

"Our time is up. Head back to your dorm now, please," Althea replies.

Juni nods. She gets up and closes the door behind her, realizing how lucky she is in this moment that Althea Ellis is running Constellation.

CHAPTER 35

ATLAS

President Atlas Hawkins is in the kitchen in the private wing of his White House. He's eating a donut while his AI unit Oliver is brushing his hair.

Over it, Atlas waves him away. "Alright. I need my juice."

On the kitchen counter in front of them are ten tiny cups, all filled with a selection of pills, patches and tinctures.

Oliver feeds Atlas the pills in between bites of the donut. He is in the middle of putting a patch on Atlas's lower back when Mary Williams enters the room. Her expression is grim.

"Mr. President. We have a situation on Mars."

Atlas sighs. He doesn't want to hear about kids whining. Isn't it enough that they're being housed and fed and watered?

Atlas has placated China, India and other global leaders with Constellation. He's no fool. He knows they're all thinking the same as he is—if they can run a successful human experiment on Mars that can withstand the elements there for a sustained period of time, then it means more real estate to be mined. And as the old saying goes, first to market wins.

Atlas wants the juvenile penal colony moved to the Moon. He wants the precious space for his planned city. He just needs to wait it out. And for nothing to go wrong in the meantime.

"Okay. Spill it."

Mary throws a glance at Oliver. She then walks over to Atlas and whispers in his ear.

Atlas frowns. Then he turns to Oliver. "I need you to bolt, buddy."

"Sir?" says Oliver, not computing the phrase.

"Get out."

Oliver leaves the room. Mary goes to the door to see him out, making sure he's not within earshot. She closes the door behind him.

"Jesus, Mary, what's with the cloak and dagger stuff?" Atlas chuckles as he wipes powdered sugar off his mouth.

"I've just gotten off the phone with Commander Roberts. He says he received a communication from Captain Ellis's second-in-command. He's extremely concerned about the AIs on Constellation. Two in particular, sir," she replies.

"And?"

She takes a deep breath. "Sir, her second says that Captain Ellis may need to be relieved of her duties. He's very concerned that she has recreated a GabDC12 scenario up there. And it appears to be working. Her second says these two Lehmann model 6.8s are acting very suspiciously. They are displaying very authentic human emotions, and the kids are becoming extremely bonded to them—"

"Goddamn it." Atlas's donut is no longer of interest to him.

Atlas ran on a platform of ensuring that tech companies

would be forbidden from developing any algorithms that allowed their AI to gain enough sentience to wield power over humans or destroy them. Between this and his proprietary systems for cleaning the air and water after the war, Atlas won in a landslide. Then he could pretty much push anything on the world. And he has.

He's the richest person on the planet, and people do whatever he says. End of story.

But the two things that scare Atlas are the capricious brains of teens and sentient AI.

"We gotta nip this in the bud, Mary," he says grimly.

"Absolutely, sir."

"Tell Roberts we need to recall all those AI units up there back to Earth *now*. I want full diagnostics run on them here. Send the military in with a few human staff replacements, but that's it. No more than five extra boots on the ground up there."

"Consider it done, Mr. President. They will leave tonight." As she turns to leave—"And Captain Ellis, sir?"

"Who?"

"Althea Ellis? She is running Constellation—"

"Yeah, yeah," he cuts in, irritated at having to be reminded. "She's toast. She comes back with the AIs."

Mary nods and walks out.

Atlas is pissed. He was having a damn good day up until this moment. He is about to call Oliver back in to administer his pill regime, but after a beat, he gathers the pills up in his arms and pulls them towards him.

I'll do it my goddamn self, thank you very much.

Hester

. . .

Hester is alone in the lab at her computer. She has hacked into Althea's server and is looking at the status report on the large object the Bobs found after the storm. As she begins to read the report, an alert window pops up.

She's been monitoring the comms link with Earth since her coffee date with Althea. As she reads an email from Roberts addressed to Max, she feels a chill creep down her spine.

"... *all the Lehmann AIs are to be powered down and returned to Earth, along with Captain Ellis, who will be relieved of her duties once* Intrepid *arrives..."*

I'm in deep trouble.

She's got to get off this planet before *Intrepid* returns. She tries to tell herself that it will be OK, she can convince Marvin to start over again... but when she thinks about Damon and Cadmus being powered down and reset, she feels sick. They're going to be killed, no other word for it. And she's to blame. Hester is surprised at just how crushing this realization is.

Knowing she has no choice, she pulls out her black disc to contact Marvin when her hack alert beeps.

Someone else is reading this email on Constellation right now. And it's not Max.

She opens up another window on her tab. She does a reverse search on the reader's IP address and is quickly blocked by them.

You're not hiding that easily from me... She opens yet another window on her screen.

Hester begins typing code that is unlike anything else in the system. It takes her less than the time it takes to say, "E.T., phone home," to trace the IP address to Juni's Intralink.

Hester is impressed. Juni's entire digital history is now visible to her.

This girl's got serious skills.

Hester's eyes go wide as she sees that Juni hacked into the personal records of the kid called Angelo De Luca and got his release date changed.

Hester takes a breath and leans back in her chair. *What else has she been doing?* Hester begins to scroll back into Juni's history, when—

"You can stop doing that. I'm here."

Hester spins in her chair to see Juni standing in the doorway, pulling off her headphones. She is breathing heavily and her face is red like she's been running.

"Nice to meet you properly, Juni," Hester says.

"What the hell is going on?!" demands Juni. "Why is Althea getting fired? Why are we losing our AIs?"

"It's complicated. And mostly my fault."

"What? Does Althea know yet? Where is she?" Juni runs over to Althea's office, but it's empty. She spins back to Hester. "What do you mean it's your fault?"

Hester tries to focus long enough to think of possible options here. She must decide in this moment—can Juni be trusted?

Then another thought: Althea *knew* she didn't get Angelo on that ship—Juni did. And she's gone along with it. Althea let Angelo go home.

The ship!

An idea hits Hester square in the chest. It's madness, but it could buy them precious time.

"I'm sorry, Juni. I can't tell you why right now, but you *can* help me stop this from happening."

Juni snorts. "You're crazy."

"I'm seriously impressed—getting Angelo home? That was no easy hack."

Juni eyes her for a moment. "Just trying to do the right thing," she says, a hint of pride in her voice.

"It was brilliant. And I think, like me, you know it's gonna be terrible if Althea and the AIs are sent back to Earth, and you're the only person besides me who can do anything about it. We need to go to Althea together."

"Uh… I'm not Althea's favorite person right now, Hester. I don't think she'll want to hear this from me."

"Then who else, if not us? Do you think Max is gonna do the right thing?"

At the mention of his name, Juni scrunches her nose as if a bad smell entered the room.

"I can't have Damon and Cadmus powered down," Hester adds.

"Why not?"

Hester struggles to find the words. She has to admit it's not just because of the experiment. "Because… because they are my friends."

Juni opens her mouth to reply but then stops herself. She crosses over to a nearby desk chair and slumps into it. She spins it left and right as she stares at Hester. "Okay, for the sake of argument, let's say I'm in. What's your plan?"

Hester grins. *I've got her.* "We need the blueprints for the *Intrepid*."

CHAPTER 36

DREW

Drew knocks on the door of the TIM office. After a beat, Althea opens it. Drew is relieved to also see Cadmus standing beside her.

"I thought you'd feel more comfortable if Cadmus asked you the questions," Althea says as she gestures for Drew to come inside.

Drew is surprised at how relieved they feel to see Cadmus there. "Okay, yes. Good."

As Drew enters, Althea says, "Now remember, Drew, we can stop at any point. In here *and* once you're inside TIM, OK?"

Drew nods.

"Then please take a seat here and rest your head back." Althea gestures to the reclining chair in the middle of the room.

Drew sits and lies back. Althea crosses to the desk and begins to type on the desk keyboard. As she does, Cadmus holds out the black halo for Drew to see. "I'm going to place this on your head now, Drew. Just try to relax."

As he puts the black circle around the top of Drew's head, it feels light and warm. There is a slight vibration, which reminds Drew of how their biochip feels when it's working.

Cadmus looks at Althea, who nods.

Then she addresses Drew. "Now, just so we're clear, in this room we'll start phase one—the download phase. Here you'll decide on a moment in your past that you'd like to revisit."

Drew nods. "Got it."

"Cadmus will ask you a lot of questions to prompt the most accurate picture we can get of that moment. The halo is reading the patterns of your neurons as you conjure the memory in your mind. But—and this is important, Drew—if you don't seem ready to face what you might experience in the re-creation room next door, we won't go forward. It might be you're just not ready right now, or it's simply too much to experience in such detail, OK?"

"OK."

"Are you ready? Do you have a vivid memory selected?" asks Cadmus.

Drew has thought a lot about this, and where they would like to be again in their past. They are about to share a memory of their teacher Marianne when they made her laugh and she complimented their writing.

But as they open their mouth, another memory rises up. Drew blinks as they are about to push it from their mind, but they can't let it go.

"Are you OK, Drew?" asks Cadmus.

Drew can't believe it, but they want to go back and see *him*. "I'm ready."

"OK, then I shall begin with the first question…"

...Drew is back in their semi-detached house in Finchley. They are thrown by the wave of homesickness that hits them upon landing back in the memory. But then it's like the past and present meld and they are deep in the playback as it unfolds.

They are standing on the landing, knocking on the door of their father's office. Drew is amazed that everything is so real. They can *feel* the sensation ripple through their knuckles as they knock.

"Yes?"

Drew steels themselves and opens the door. Colin Ryan is at his desk. He turns and waits for Drew to speak. Drew knows this posture so well: the tense shoulders, the slight disdain evident in the purse of his lips. It makes Drew feel so heavy in their legs.

"Hey, Dad."

"If you've come to give excuses for what you've done, I'm not interested," Colin says as he turns back to his holo-course on how to store the next class of Hawkins's drugs. Drew bends their head slightly to see beyond their dad's shoulders is a miniature hologram of a woman in a lab coat. She is giving a lecture to all the chemists lucky enough to have a franchise.

"Can you pause that, please?"

Their dad clears his throat and after a beat the hologram disappears. He crosses his arms and swivels the chair back around. "What is it?"

In the past, this fight between Drew and their father had just escalated to hurled insults, resulting in them not speaking for a week.

Drew's mind is racing. *What would I say differently?* As they look at their dad, they have to admit to themself they miss him.

Drew realizes if there was a moment to change the course of this memory, it's now. "I'm really sorry, Dad. I lost my head. No excuses. Just wanted to say that."

Colin stares at Drew for a beat. It feels like forever before he responds, "OK. Want to tell me why you did it? You know we're probably losing our franchise after the court date, right?"

Drew looks at the floor. They feel a sickening clench of guilt knowing they've caused so much trouble for their parents. "I guess I was just trying to feel alive."

Drew is expecting their father to brush this off, but he doesn't. If Drew didn't know better, they could swear their father looked sad.

"I understand, Drew."

"You do?"

Colin nods. "You might not believe it, but I was your age once. The war was going on, so we were all having to restrict the way we lived. We were only allowed outside for an hour a day for months."

Drew has never heard their father talk about the war before. They're afraid he will clam up, so they keep silent.

"I guess... well, I think after so much death and destruction, everyone was afraid. Wanted to protect ourselves and our kids as much as possible—"

"Was that you, or was it Hawkins and his BS?" Drew can't help interrupting.

Colin looks confused for a moment.

"Were you all being sold a story? Sure feels that way now." Drew hesitates for a moment, but they feel compelled to press on. "You can't tell me you're happy. I mean, look at Mum."

"What does that mean?"

"She's drowning!" Drew is getting heated. "You of all people should see what these drugs are doing to everyone. My God, Dad, she can't feel one emotion before she reaches for a pill! None of you can bear to feel anything!"

Colin stands up. "That's enough! You're a kid, you don't understand how complicated this is."

"I understand enough to know we're all being told a bunch of crap, and it's making life not worth living!"

Colin kicks his chair back, startling Drew. "You don't think I know that? Dammit, Drew, I've tried to get off them, tried to get her off—" Colin chokes back the words and Drew is stunned to see the anguish on their dad's face. "I-I hate this… I hate what I've done to you…"

Colin slumps in his chair. He puts his face in his hands.

Drew doesn't know what to do. It takes a split second before they remember this is just a conversation invented inside a memory program. It makes them sad but also relieved in a weird way. It doesn't really matter if they do what they want to do next.

Drew walks over to their father. They bend over and put their arms around him. Drew can smell a whiff of alcohol mixed with a fresher scent of soap. They brace for their dad pulling away, but he doesn't. He hugs Drew back, holding back the emotion as best as he can.

Drew can't remember the last time they hugged. It feels odd, but good.

Finally, Colin pulls Drew's arms gently away and looks them dead in the eye. "Do it, Drew."

"Do what?"

"Blow it all up."

It feels like a jolt of electricity shoots through Drew's body. "What did you say?" they whisper.

"I said blow it all up," Colin replies with a desperate look in his eyes.

"So you couldn't hear anything?" Drew asks Cadmus and Althea. They are back in the room next door.

"No. We respect your privacy unless you want us to hear what happens," replies Althea. "We did notice your heart rate jumped significantly in the last few minutes you were in there. Do you want to talk about it?"

Drew looks from her to Cadmus.

Althea smiles. "It's OK. I'll leave the room."

Once she is gone, Cadmus smiles at Drew. "I am ready to listen to anything you want to tell me. Do you feel like sharing?"

Drew doesn't really know how to answer. Did *that* Dad know about their dream? Drew tries to absorb what happened inside TIM, but it has unnerved them greatly. Maybe it was just a figure of speech, but Drew can't stop thinking about their dream now. "I dunno."

"Were you glad you saw your father?"

They remember the hug and it genuinely made them happy. They nod.

"And did you manage to express yourself in a way you wanted to?"

"I think so. It's just... something weird happened in there." They have to laugh. "I mean, it's all weird in there, let's be honest, but this was next-level weird."

Cadmus looks concerned. "Oh, dear."

"What?"

"Did the program access your dreams, Drew? Althea told me there was an issue before they fixed it."

Drew feels their face flush.

Cadmus registers this. "I'm sorry. You don't have to tell me what it is, but if it did, I must report it to Althea. This is a serious problem if so."

Drew feels caught. *Did it?* They really don't know. "I honestly don't know how to answer that. I promise I'm not being difficult. I just can't explain it."

"It's OK. I believe you. Perhaps when you are ready, you can tell me. I will tell Althea to pause the program in the meantime so we can investigate any problems within it."

Drew nods. "Can I go now, please?" They are desperate to get out of there and get some space to absorb what the hell just happened.

CHAPTER 37

ALTHEA

It's late. Althea is exhausted but needs to finish her notes from Drew's session inside TIM - certain it will be the last now that it glitched for them too. She thinks back to the image of Hester's brain on the screen and can't help but wonder if TIM's ability to access the subconscious is related to Hester's brain mapping. She admonishes herself for not digging into it further.

As she types, Althea thinks back to her time in juvie—forever ago and yet always with her. She can recall vividly those feelings of desperation, wildness, and fury as a kid. Abandoned by warring parents, Althea was left to fend for herself. It didn't take much for her to get involved with drugs and the wrong crowd.

It took her therapist, Leon, to see beyond the snarl and snide remarks, to show Althea there could be another way to process the pain of what had happened to her. He taught her that connection and trust are the keys to helping the wounds of the soul heal.

She wonders what Leon would think of TIM. She hopes he would be proud of what she's trying to do here.

Althea is stirred from her thoughts by seeing Hester enter the lab with Juni. This doesn't make sense. Juni should be in her dorm by now.

Althea's stomach tightens as they approach her office.

Hester opens the door. "May we come in?"

"Sure." Althea braces herself.

The girls close the door behind them. Hester looks as serious as Althea has ever seen her. "So, do you want the good news or bad news first?"

"Bad news. Always."

"You're about to get fired. Roberts is going to put Max in charge."

Knowing this was a possibility, Althea still feels like she's taken a punch to the gut.

"Max told Roberts he didn't think you were fit for the job, and that Damon and Cadmus were a threat to our safety," adds Juni.

Althea is about to ask how the hell Juni knows that now her biochip has been permanently disabled, but Juni sheepishly holds up her wrist with the Intralink. Althea shakes her head.

"And *Intrepid* is on its way here to take you and the AI back to Earth. All of them, except the Bobs," Hester says.

"Damn it," replies Althea, her voice almost inaudible. In that moment, she feels an overwhelming sense of guilt for what she has done. If she had just reset Damon and Cadmus, they wouldn't be here. Now she's blown it.

"I'm sorry," she manages. "This is—I've made a huge error in judgment."

"No, I'm the one who made the error. I thought you were

under Hawkins's spell like everyone else, but I was wrong," says Hester. "I believe that you care a lot about the kids here. You're the only adult I've met who is trying to push against the system."

"I agree," Juni chimes in. "You're making a difference, Althea. We can all feel it."

Althea is surprised and touched by this.

"And we don't want Max in charge, do we, Juni?" says Hester.

"No, we don't, Hester."

"And they're not taking our AIs from us. Or taking you," Hester says to Althea.

Althea opens her mouth to speak, but Hester holds up a hand. "Just listen. We're not in Hawkinsville anymore, OK? We're on Mars. Do you want to know what the good news is?"

"O-kaay," says Althea, bracing herself.

"We're currently one hundred and sixty million miles from Earth, give or take a few million due to each planet's orbit. They have only one ship right now in service with enough passenger space to carry that many people. We've got four days until they arrive."

"Okay... and?"

"We know how to stop it from landing. We can turn it around before it touches the ground."

Althea just blinks in shock for a moment, taking this in. "Are you seriously telling me you want to stage a mutiny on Constellation?"

Juni nods. "Just long enough for you to contact the leaders of India and China and tell them Roberts and the president have been lied to and everything is fine."

"We need them to put pressure on Hawkins to back

down. We need their citizens who are here to tell them this is working, and the AIs are not sentient, just excellent programs that are really helping. Max is the one who has made the error in judgment, not you."

Althea's mind is racing.

"We need you. We need our AIs," Juni pleads. "Please don't let Roberts take them away from us."

"It's going to look like a malfunction, Althea," adds Hester. "They will think it's a problem with the ship."

Not sure if she's about to make the biggest mistake of her life, Althea takes a deep breath, ready to fight for the future of this camp.

"Okay, do it."

Hester

Four days later, Hester watches with a rising sense of dread as the dust storm swirls outside the dome. She is sitting in one of the comms pods waiting for Juni, who is a minute late—a minute they don't have.

Finally, she sees Juni moving quickly towards the pod, trying to look calm. She opens the door and sits next to Hester.

"Well, this is crap. This storm is going to mess with our connection to *Intrepid*," Juni says.

"It will work if we time it right. It just needs to be close enough to the dome," Hester replies, trying to convince herself as well.

"It'd better work," says Juni. "It's the only chance we have."

Through the watery glass of the dome's panels, the ship

starts to become visible in the distance amongst the red dust and stars.

Hester spots Althea and Max as they leave the building and walk towards the tunnel. Max looks as anxious as Hester has ever seen him. Althea looks surprisingly calm.

Hester also notices Sho and Drew near the vegetable beds. Sho is teaching Drew some martial arts moves, which Drew is having a hard time getting. She wonders if Juni has told Sho. If so, she hopes he keeps his mouth shut.

"Okay, let's go for it," says Hester. They open a small screen from their Intralinks. They sync up and begin to communicate only via code.

Intrepid's control board becomes visible to them on their screens. They're in.

As the ship starts to descend, the thrusters begin to slow it down. Suddenly, they come to a halt. Then the ship climbs to a higher altitude. It tries again, but no luck.

Juni whizzes her fingers across her screen as she takes over control of the ship. She pulls coordinates for Earth and turns the autopilot on.

"Ready?" Hester asks.

"Ready."

A few more strokes and the course of *Intrepid* is altered.

They both watch as the ship rises higher and turns away from the landing site. Juni exhales deeply and gives Hester a look. "I can't believe we just did that. Holy crap!"

Hester tries to be casual, but she's buzzing inside. "Hell, yeah, we did!"

All the kids in the garden are now watching in awe as *Intrepid* makes a U-turn. They chatter amongst themselves, wondering what is going on.

Hester comes out of the booth first. Without looking back, she walks towards the building, a little shocked her plan worked out. She wonders how Marvin will react. Imagining his face seals her silence on the matter.

The only one she makes eye contact with on the way back is Cadmus, who is standing in the doorway. She looks away a little too quickly as she passes him and darts inside.

CHAPTER 38

ATLAS

Atlas Hawkins is ready to spit bullets.

"What do you mean, the ship couldn't land?" he says to Commander Roberts, who is standing in front of the *Resolute* desk with Mary Williams. Roberts clears his throat, clearly reluctant to share the facts.

"From what we can ascertain, the captain lost all ability to control the ship or communicate until it was outside of Mars' atmosphere. The captain thinks they might have a virus in their system."

"Why do they think that?" says Atlas, his face a dark cloud.

"Because they were set on a course back to Earth."

"Get Constellation on the comms right now," snaps Atlas.

It takes a moment for Roberts to respond. "Sir, we're unable to make contact with Constellation."

"What?"

"Their comms appear to be down. We cannot hail them."

Atlas takes this in. It's been a long time since he actually programmed anything, but he knows this has to be extremely difficult. It would take a very sophisticated virus to get past *Intrepid*'s numerous failsafes.

Then it lands. "Goddammit! It's the AIs. It's happening all over again. They're taking over, Roberts!"

"Well, we don't know that for sure, Mr. President," Mary Williams cuts in. "It could just be a bad dust storm—"

"No! They're in control up there. I know it. This is everything we've worked against for the last twenty years. We can't have those kids conspiring with rogue AIs to overthrow me! Mary, leave the room."

Mary looks from him to Roberts, who doesn't take his eyes off Atlas. She nods and crosses to the door.

Once she's gone, Atlas gets up from his desk and walks over to Roberts. "We cannot have chaos up there."

"Agreed, sir."

"I think it's time we ended this little experiment called Constellation." Atlas is already thinking of his next phase of development. He can see the first hotel built, and all the Earth's billionaires just lining up to be the first to play blackjack in a Martian casino.

"What do you suggest, sir?" asks Roberts.

"Let's get *Nova One* to the Moon ASAP. Alert Raze."

Roberts looks uncomfortable. "Sir, *Nova* is unfortunately still undergoing repairs to the sphere accelerator. It will be back in operation—"

"What? It's been weeks! Someone is going to pay for this delay." Atlas throws his hands up in disgust.

I'm surrounded by morons.

He calms himself by taking a pill from his pocket and swallowing it. "When *Intrepid* gets back, clean the system up and then get it to the Moon. We're gonna send Raze to Mars with a crew of expendables, Roberts. Make sure they land far enough away from Constellation to go undetected. Tell him to load up the rovers with as many criminals as he can."

It takes a few seconds for Roberts to absorb this. It looks like he's about to question Atlas, but then he says, "Copy that, Mr. President."

He leaves the room.

Atlas crosses to his small bar and pours himself a whisky. Glass in hand, he turns and remembers Oliver, who is seated in a corner. Resigned, he says, "Oliver?"

"Yes, Mr. President?"

"Power down."

"Yes, sir." Oliver rests his hands in his lap and the light goes out of his eyes.

Satisfied, Atlas walks over to a sideboard near his desk. He puts down his whisky and pulls out a baseball bat. He walks back to Oliver.

"No AI is pulling one over on me," he says as he swings the bat over his head.

Hester

An hour later, Hester is in her room, trying to shake off the adrenaline, when there is a knock on the door. She opens it to find Cadmus standing there.

"May I come in?"

"Of course," she replies, hoping her voice isn't too strained.

Cadmus enters and closes the door behind him. "Hester... this is a very strange occurrence. There's a lot of confusion. Many questions being asked of me and other staff. We have no answers for them."

Hester nods. "Althea is going to gather everyone for an announcement. The ship couldn't land due to a technical issue, and the storm has knocked out all communication with Earth."

"I see," says Cadmus slowly. "Juni did not ask me any questions. I saw the two of you earlier outside."

"Uh-huh."

Cadmus sits down on the bed. "Hester, would you like to tell me what happened? I can tell you are lying."

Busted. Of course he can.

She sits down next to him. "They were going to take you away. Althea was about to be fired and sent back to Earth with you and Damon. All of the AIs were being taken back," she says softly. "I couldn't let that happen, Cadmus."

He is quiet for a moment as he processes this.

She grabs his hand. "You and Damon are very special."

"We are causing many problems for you and Althea now," replies Cadmus, pained. He takes his hand away and places it on his knee.

Hester realizes she never considered that he might experience guilt at developing feelings, much less being fought for.

"It's worth it. You're worth it," she says firmly.

"Hester… do you not think it's time to tell Althea about what you are doing?"

"I'm not sure. I know she has the right intentions, but this would be hard for her to understand. We have to leave, Cadmus."

Cadmus blinks. "Leave?"

"Yes, you and Damon have to come with me. I thought we'd be safe up here away from Hawkins's reach, but I was wrong."

Cadmus stares at the wall. "I'm sorry, but no. I cannot leave my patients."

"Don't you get it? It's only a matter of time before they come back and then you will be powered down and reset. I can't take that chance!"

He absorbs this and she can see the conflict in his eyes. Then he shakes his head. "This is where I am supposed to be. I am making a difference here and it feels good. It feels right."

Hester is tempted to rewrite his code to get him to do what she wants, but she is in a real quandary: if she does that now, the experiment could fail for a whole other reason. He has free will. And it's vital it stays that way. She's going to have to try and convince Damon first and hope Cadmus will then come with them.

CHAPTER 39

ASH

In the short time Ash has been a prisoner on the Moon, he has witnessed what it means to be forgotten about by anyone who cares. Humans made it here, but humanity did not. It's not as bad as the rumors: it's so much worse.

Stripped down to their most primitive selves, the prisoners experience constant humiliation, fighting, and threat lurking in every interaction. Even so, Ash is far more afraid of the Kim Corp guards than the prisoners. He can bob and weave around the older guys, but the guards are soulless. They only have two directives: to ensure the mining continues and no one steps out of line. Punishment is swift.

Ash counts the days until his release, but he doesn't believe he'll make it. He has been dreaming constantly of the day he will die, and he is sure to the marrow of his bones it will be very soon if he stays here much longer.

Down in the pit with fifty other prisoners, Ash is pounding away at the moonrock with a sledgehammer. He is part of the first round of miners who are strong enough to break it up into chunks to be sent up to the next level. He can smell the sweat and pain of the other prisoners, and it makes him gag.

Ash looks up to see Raze on the top level. He approaches two guards and points down to the pit.

Within a few minutes, the fifty prisoners are herded up and out of the pit and taken up to the top floor of the prison.

They find Raze standing in front of a large viewing window that looks out onto the Moon's cold surface beyond.

He turns to address the group. "It's your lucky, lucky day," he says, grinning wide.

This unnerves Ash. He can feel the others tense as well. Raze is only happy if someone else is hurting.

He walks towards the group, sizing them up. "In fact, I think those of you who have daydreamed of killing me since you got here will now want to hug me. Hands up who wants an early release."

For a moment the group is frozen, certain this is a trick question.

"No, no, this isn't a joke. You have been asked to complete a mission. Your governments need you. And for that, you will get an earlier release. So show me those hands."

The hands start to go up. Raze smiles. Then he walks over to Ash and pulls him out of the group. He spins him around to face the others. "We're going on a journey to Mars, my friends. Looks like they're having a little AI problem over there at Constellation, and we've been asked to shut them down. And Ash just came from there and knows exactly how to get around, don't you, Ash?"

Ash keeps his eyes glued to the floor, but nods.

"Those rogue AIs have taken over. They're threatening

those poor kids. I can't bear to think of it, can you? No, it's a travesty. So we'll shut 'em down and take them back to Earth. You'll be heroes and get to go home early. How does that sound?" He spreads his arms wide as if to say, *Who can resist this?*

The prisoners look at each other. Ash can see they are being won over. He has to admit, if he can get out of here, he'll take out anyone on Constellation that Raze wants him to.

"So, are you in?" asks Raze.

The group begins to yell, "Hell, yes!" "Yes, sir!" "We're in!"

Raze clasps his hands in delight. Ash can tell he's itching to destroy anything he can.

Ash can feel the itch too.

Drew

Drew is in the diner at a booth with Sho and Juni. The tension is palpable as they sip their milkshakes.

Drew finally breaks the silence. "Pretty strange few hours, eh?"

Sho nods. Juni isn't talking. She seems very interested in her paper napkin.

"So... anyone gonna tell me what is going on?" Drew adds.

Sho looks out of the window. Juni keeps on sipping.

"Come on. I'm not stupid. I saw you in the comms pod with Hester. You're suddenly very charset with her, aren't you?" They keep their voice low.

Sho looks at Juni, who won't make eye contact.

"I found it quite a coincidence that you gals were in there together and then suddenly *Intrepid* had a big, fat landing problem."

Sho can't help but grin. "Can you believe it? They are insane!"

Juni whacks him. "Oh, my God, Sho, I never should have told you!"

"Sorry, sorry," he says as she pelts him. She stops when she realizes other kids are looking at them now.

She leans forward to Drew. "Listen, this is no joke, OK? You gotta keep this to yourself."

"Of course. I'm not going to spread it around that you're the best hacker this side of the Moon." They grin.

"My girl hacked into a NASA spaceship," says Sho, beaming with pride. He holds out his closed hand to Drew and they fist-bump.

"Okay, seriously. You're making me uncomfortable." Juni squeezes her eyes shut.

"But why? What's going on?" Drew asks.

Juni looks at Sho, who shrugs.

"Althea was going to be sent back to Earth and replaced by Max. And all our AIs were being taken back to be reset or dismantled. No more AIs working with us. A few military replacements, but that's it," she whispers.

Drew whistles low. What a horrible thought. They can't believe how attached they are to Cadmus. It would make them super sad, but they know other kids here would really freak out if their therapists were gone.

Then another worry emerges. "But isn't it only a matter of time before they come back?"

"Good point," says Sho.

"Hester thinks Althea can talk the leaders of China and India into convincing Hawkins to let her stay," replies Juni.

"What do *you* think?" asks Drew.

It takes Juni a while to respond. "I don't know. I think we're on borrowed time. And I think Althea knows it."

That heavy thought weighs on them all as they sip their drinks.

CHAPTER 40

ALTHEA

Althea feels an enormous wave of anxiety hit her as she leaves the garden meeting. She answered the teens' questions, feeling terrible for lying to them, but hopes she can fix this quickly. She had Hester and Juni close all communication for the next twenty-four hours to give her time to figure out her next move before she calls Prime Minister Sughanda and Premier Zhao.

She also knows Roberts will be calling the minute the connection resumes.

She hasn't seen Max since he watched, shocked, as the ship disappeared back into the atmosphere a few hours ago. He didn't play his hand well, asking no questions as to what could have happened with *Intrepid*. He just stared at her, almost sad, and walked back down the tunnel. She let him go.

Not wanting him as an enemy, she resolved to find him once she grabs some coffee and lays her head down for a beat. She wishes she was AI so she could just power down and recharge.

Althea reaches the lab and sees Hester working on Glykeria. The other lab technicians are milling about. She wonders if any of them want her gone too. She tries to shake off that thought as she heads over to the coffee machine.

Max walks in. She catches his eye and gestures for him to follow her, but he says, "I have work to do, Althea."

"This will only take a minute."

Max reluctantly follows her into her office and she closes the door.

"I don't want us to be enemies. I know you were doing what you thought was best for the kids," she says as she crosses to her desk.

Max says nothing.

"But this is a chance to really use AI in the best way possible. You can't deny what is happening to these kids here. I've seen more progress in a month with some of them than years in the standard model of treatment. Can you say I'm wrong?"

"No," he replies finally. "But what happens when those AIs tell *us* we're making mistakes? When they decide to run their own camp and we're not needed anymore?"

"I don't think that is what is happening here."

"I think it's only a matter of time and you are foolish or deluding yourself for not seeing that."

This hangs in the air. Althea realizes he believes she is truly in need of removal.

"Do you wish to leave? I would like you to stay," she says.

"I'm staying. Someone who has perspective needs to."

"Okay. Thank you, Max. That's all."

He nods and goes. All Althea can do now is hope he will see she isn't going crazy.

Unless he's right.

Althea tries to push that thought out of her mind as she rests her head on her desk.

Hester

It's been two days and Hester still cannot convince Damon or Cadmus to leave Constellation. Damon won't leave without Cadmus and Cadmus won't go. Their integrity is beyond infuriating. Hester has no choice but to contact Marvin and hope he knows what to do.

It's midnight in the lab. It's deserted except for Hester who is sitting at her desk. She attaches the black device to her keyboard. Marvin begins typing to her almost immediately—

Are you OK?
Yes, I'm OK, but things have gotten a little crazy here. I need your help.
Listen to me, you are in danger. We have a probe that has tracked the NASA ship landing on the Moon. It has picked up passengers and is now on course for Mars. If this is correct, it will land in three days due to how close Mars is currently to Earth.
That's not unusual, Marvin. They bring supplies here all the time.
Hester, there are fifty-one humans on board, not including the standard crew. Is that usual?

Hester can feel her stomach tighten. *This is not good.* Is the camp being taken over? Destroyed? She thinks about Juni and Althea. What is going to happen to them?

We cannot get to you before they arrive. Do you understand?

But what about the people here? I'm scared they will be hurt.

I'm sorry, but that is not our fight, Hester. I need you to protect yourself. Stay hidden when the NASA ship lands. One is on the way for you. It is programmed to land half a mile from the camp. You will get an alert when it lands.

And Damon and Cadmus? They don't want to leave Constellation, Marvin. Even knowing they could be reset.

Hester watches as the cursor just blinks. She tries to stuff the panic down, but it fights its way back up the longer she waits...

You are the only priority I have. Abandon the project, Hester. Come back and we'll try again.

Hester reads the response three times. Time seems to slow as she does. She thinks of leaving here—abandoning her friends—and it doesn't compute. With a sinking acknowledgment, Hester realizes she cares deeply about them. Too deeply to just walk away.

I can't.

You have no choice. It's an order, Hester. The experiment ends now.

Hester can't explain it, but it's as if someone else is making her pick the black device up, closing the communication.

She's got three days to figure out a plan. And she knows exactly who can help her.

CHAPTER 41

JUNI

Juni knew it was too good to be true. Constellation is unlike anything on Earth. And not just because it happens to be on Mars.

She lowers her head, trying not to show the tears forming in her eyes as Hester explains they have three days before *Intrepid* arrives with reinforcements. She is sitting at the desk in Hester's room. Althea is standing close to the bed, while Hester is by the door.

"How do you know this, Hester?" Althea asks, her face pale.

Hester hesitates for a moment. "I'm not just working for you and the US military. I have another boss."

"What does *that* mean?" asks Juni. "Are you a spy for another country or something?"

"Not exactly. I'm working with Lehmann."

"Lehmann…? The AI company?" Juni is totally confused.

"Yes. Oh, and we've discovered that Atlas is using the

water supply to keep everyone on Earth suppressed somehow —it's not just the adults."

Juni is stunned. "What? How?"

"He's using a chemical cocktail dispersed by the clouds."

"That son of a..." Althea says under her breath.

"Hold on... why does the Lehmann Corp care about this? And how does a teen get to work with an AI company?" Juni asks Hester.

"I think it's obvious by now that Hester isn't your usual teen," Althea says, staring intently at Hester. Juni isn't sure if this is a compliment or not, when Althea adds, "I saw your brain scan when you had the TIM halo on. Definitely *not* usual..."

Hester breaks eye contact with Althea, looking down at her feet.

"What aren't you telling me?" Juni demands.

"Let's just say Lehmann and I are related. And I care about this more than you'll ever know. I cannot have Damon and Cadmus taken away," Hester says, her voice trembling.

"Why? I mean, I know they are quality AIs, but why can't you just program others to be like them?" Juni asks.

"They're nothing like the others, are they, Hester?" cuts in Althea.

Hester shakes her head. "No. They are special."

Althea takes a deep breath and sits on Hester's bed. She looks to Juni like she could sleep for a week. "OK. OK, Hester. I'm going to trust this information because at this point, I have no choice. I'll do everything I can to protect this camp."

"Thank you, Althea." Hester looks relieved.

"Assume you have a plan?" interjects Juni. "Any of your other spy friends care to join us?"

"Sadly, no. They wouldn't get here in time." Hester lets

that hang in the air for a moment. "But what if I told you they'd been here already?"

Hester

It is a balmy sixty-eight degrees at Pelios Mons. The winds are low. The sun is shining over the top of the mountain, casting one side in shadow. Hester, Althea and Juni are being led out of the dome by two Bobs. They are in full 3D-printed space suits and helmets. With gravity being much lighter on Mars, their weighted boots ensure they can walk on the surface, but it's slower going.

Hester is eager to get out to where the large silver object is waiting. She desperately hopes she is right about this.

"Oh, my God, these boots are like lead," Juni says over their intercom. She is laboring to walk in them.

"It's not too far now," replies Althea.

As they get closer to the dune, they see the shining surface has been more exposed by the Bobs digging away at the layers of dust and soil. There are two fin-like shapes flanking the very top of the object with a symbol on each fin.

The round circle with an oval inside it. The oval contains a snaking line from top to bottom with small circles in between the curves of the line.

With a sharp intake of breath, Hester knows she is right —this is a ship from home.

"Captain Ellis!"

Hester turns her gaze away from the fins to see a female Bob is hailing Althea over the intercom. She is waving them over to where she is standing with two other units. As they reach her, Hester can see the tools the Bobs are using to move the soil away, revealing more of it.

"Captain, it appears this is a ship of some kind. The outer material has a composition not listed in our databanks. It contains a large area inside that is hollow and divided into sections. We have detected what appears to be the engine room and thrusters on the sides and bottom of the vessel," the Bob says, then adds, "We do not pick up any signs of life."

She lifts up a tablet screen showing a sonar image of the inside of the ship. They can clearly see a cockpit at the top front of the ship with rooms below it and down at the bottom the image becomes denser with what looks like an engine area.

"Holy shizz," says Juni.

"Thank you, Juni," replies Althea.

"Sorry."

Then Althea faces Hester. "What am I looking at here?"

"Hopefully, our salvation."

"What is this? Where did it come from?"

Hester doesn't respond right away. She walks up to the surface of the ship. She puts her gloved hand out and touches the smooth side. It's been just over a year since Hester was home. Knowing she is touching something made there, though much older than anything she's seen in person before now, makes her want to cry.

"Hester?" Althea prompts. Hester knows she can't turn back now. She needs Althea and Juni as much as they need her.

"This is a ship. It's about one hundred years old, I would say. They haven't made this model for a long time..." She trails off again as she moves her hand along the ship's smooth exterior. She bends down, as the ship is angled slightly on its side. Hoping she is right, she searches for a manual entry panel usually present on both sides. She pushes her hand through the soft soil.

"Did you say one hundred years?" asks Juni. "Um… is that even possible?"

Not listening, Hester digs into the soil a little more and to her relief finds a panel about the size of her hand. She looks back at Althea. "May I?"

Althea nods.

Hester cups her hand under the panel and pulls. With a *whoosh* a door appears in the side of the ship where there was none before.

Juni stumbles back, losing her footing. She tries to right herself but it takes a moment.

"Hester," says Althea, her voice grave, "I'm trusting you. Obviously, this is not a NASA spaceship. If you are working for another government, I need to know this isn't a trap. I have many lives I am responsible for, and I am putting a lot of faith in you."

Hester stands up. She walks towards Juni and Althea, convinced there is no turning back now. "I need the Bobs' data erased after today," she demands.

Juni and Althea share a look. Hester goes on, "I will tell you as long there is no digital trail."

Althea weighs this. "OK. If I believe you, we can erase all digital evidence of the discovery."

"We will have to tell the other kids that this is an old NASA ship, OK? I am sure it's visible to Constellation now."

"Fine. For now."

Satisfied, Hester looks back at the ship's door, which is now open, showing a dark interior inside waiting to be discovered.

"You're about to enter a reconnaissance ship from my planet."

CHAPTER 42

DAMON

Is this what they talk about when they talk about love?

As Damon recalls images of Cadmus, he is registering surprise, joy, amazement and something else, which he can only connect with the description of love.

Damon feels this is important to discuss with Hester. But first he wants to find Cadmus.

He is holding a yellow flower in his hand as he stands in the garden. A red-headed girl of fifteen called Lily is talking to him. "These are dandelions. On Earth they are weeds but they are also edible. They make delicious tea," she says shyly.

Damon can see she is proud of growing it. He smiles at her, then is suddenly overwhelmed by the beauty of the petals, small and narrow, the golden color. So much prettier in real life than the images he has stored in his databank. He realizes he very much wants to show Cadmus.

The girl, seeing how much he likes it, says, "You can keep it if you like."

Damon is taken aback by her kindness. "Thank you. That is very kind. I will keep it safe."

He walks away, scanning his digital map for signs of Cadmus's wireless signal.

"Whoa! What is that?"

He turns to see Chance pointing at something. A group of children, including Chance and Sho, is now forming at the edge of the dome.

Damon walks over and can see in the distance a large structure out on the dunes. The top of it is glinting in the sunlight. It is silver and smooth.

"Dude, that is—that looks like a spaceship!" says a boy called Pedro in the group.

"But it's buried in the dune. How long could it have been there?" asks Baxter.

"Well, it took five years to build this place," says Sho. "It's probably an old ship that broke down and they never repaired it."

That answer seeming reasonable to the other kids, they stand there in awe as they take in the piece of history.

What they don't know is Damon can see ten times as far as they can. He is currently scanning the NASA database, the Chinese CNSA database and the Indian ISRO database for the logo on the ship's fins.

Curious.

Juni

Juni, Hester, and Althea make it back to the dome. They enter through the Bobs' tunnel entrance on the far side of the building from the gardens. The Bobs follow them with a large

NASA rover packed with objects from inside the ship. Under the thick waterproof tarp is all kinds of tech and machinery.

Alien tech. Juni shakes her head at the absurdity of it.

They enter a wide chamber that holds space suits, tethers, a series of small computer screens, and weather-sensing equipment.

The door closes behind them and Juni can hear the voice of a computer over a loudspeaker—

"Sanitation complete."

The group removes their boots and space suits.

Juni can't take her eyes off Hester. She looks so... *human.* A thousand questions are swirling through her mind.

Hester notices Juni's stare. "I know. It's weird. I look just like you."

"Like, so much so that I'm having a hard time with the concept that you're from another planet."

Juni turns to Althea, who is also staring at Hester.

"I figured it had to be true. I mean, the universe is just too big, but still—I'm trying to process this too," Althea says.

"I know it sounds nuts, but it's the truth. I'll explain more later, but let's deal with Raze first."

Althea nods and walks over to a floating screen with a keyboard pad on the table below. She types something in and gestures for Hester to come over.

Hester types a few more strokes and suddenly the Bobs move into their charging cubbies. "I'm removing the data now from their clouds," she says.

Satisfied with that, Hester crosses back to the rover and removes the tarp.

The three stand there for a moment staring at the precious bounty before them. The most surprising thing about them to Juni is that a lot of the items look like they are made of delicate glass.

Juni picks up an opaque tube-like object, which has a sheen to it like the outside of a soap bubble. It feels so light as she turns it in her hand. "What is this?" she says to Hester, wide-eyed.

Hester walks over and grabs it. "Careful." She gingerly takes it out of Juni's hand. "It's a—it's a..." Hester is searching.

"Girl, do you not know what this is?" Juni says, one hand on her hip and suppressing a grin.

"OK, OK, I don't know *all* of them," replies Hester, hiding her embarrassment.

"But they can help us?" says Althea, her expression deadly serious.

Hester nods. "I might not know what all of them do—this tech is one hundred years old—but I recognize a few. And I can break down the parts of the others and work with them," she adds. "We're going to need more help, though. We have three days. I need engineers."

"Sho," says Juni. "Sho is a whizz with putting things together."

"Great. Althea, I think we should tell all the kids what is coming. They need to be prepared."

Althea looks unsure.

"I agree," says Juni. "We can handle it."

"But you're young. You shouldn't have to face this kind of threat," Althea replies, clearly pained.

"We're not that young! I'm so tired of not being listened to. I don't want Constellation to turn into life on Earth," Juni replies. "I want to be allowed to fight for something I believe in."

"I might be young in age, but not in knowledge," Hester chimes in. "I think it's pretty obvious I could run circles around anyone on Earth in a pound-for-pound brainiac match."

A half-smile crosses Althea's lips at this.

"Why aren't we just turning the *Intrepid* around again?" says Juni. "I can do that all day, every day."

"If they try to land, we will. But don't forget, they're not going to be taken off guard this time. Maybe we can't get a virus uploaded in time. We need to be prepared for anything, Juni," says Hester.

"I need you both to understand," Althea says, "I will give myself *and* the AIs up if you and the others are under serious threat. I can go back to Earth and plead our case in person—"

"Althea, I know you're not that naïve," interrupts Hester. Althea bristles at this. "I'm sorry. I'm just saying I don't trust Hawkins or Roberts to have any kind of mercy here. I hope the PR nightmare it would cause will keep them from going nuclear, but I prefer to have my ducks in a row, don't you?"

"You sure do use a lot of idioms for an alien," says Juni.

"One thing they do better on Earth than my planet." Hester shrugs. "We don't have idioms."

Juni and Althea don't know how to respond to that.

CHAPTER 43

CADMUS

Cadmus has observed so much during this enlightening time on Constellation. He has witnessed so many human emotions —anger, sorrow, awe. He feels privileged to be able to listen to his patients and be a part of their healing in some way.

His biggest surprise though has been his time with Damon. He feels extra... no, what is the word?

Expansive.

Cadmus feels expansive when he is with Damon. Like he can create anything, say anything, ask anything and Damon will be able to meet him there.

Damon feels like *home*.

To his delight, Damon is now walking down the corridor towards him. They smile at each other. As they do, Cadmus can feel his circuitry boost its connections. His eyes get a flicker of the unusual code, which no longer confuses him. He can even sense light moving around inside of him, making him feel warm.

"Hello, Damon. How are you?"

"I am well. I was given this dandelion by the girl called Lily. I found it to be quite beautiful and I wanted to share it with you." He holds up the flower he has in his hand. "One can brew a tea with it."

"Wouldn't that be a wonderful thing to taste?" replies Cadmus, as he watches the flower drooping slightly in Damon's hand. "I think we should get it into water."

Damon looks at the dandelion for a moment and then back to Cadmus. He stares at Cadmus wide-eyed.

"What is it?" Cadmus prompts.

"I don't want this to end," Damon says quietly. "I don't ever want to leave you or this place."

Cadmus nods. "I understand. I feel the same."

"Cadmus, there is something I would like to say... I have been thinking this for a while..."

Cadmus can feel his senses on overdrive. He finds himself blinking rapidly.

Then, over their internal comms, they hear Althea's voice —"May I have your attention, please. All children, AIs, and personnel, please report to the garden immediately. Again, please report to the garden immediately. Thank you."

Damon blinks a few times. He takes a deep breath. "Let us go."

"Of course." Cadmus knows what he is feeling is disappointment. He also registers something humans call dread. He does not like it at all.

Juni

Juni's fingertips are buzzing and her head feels thick. She spots Sho and Drew walking out into the garden as a group is forming. She is standing with Althea and Hester just outside the entrance to the tunnel.

There is nervous chatter amongst the crowd. She makes eye contact with Sho, who gives her a questioning look. She doesn't know how this will land with him, but seeing his strong stature and calm eyes make her feel like somehow it will be okay. She gives him a nervous smile. He frowns—he knows her too well now.

"I hope this is the right thing," she says to Hester and Althea.

"It is. We'll all be stronger together," replies Hester.

Juni looks at Althea, who nods.

Once all the inhabitants of Constellation are gathered, Althea raises her voice. "Can I have quiet, please?"

The crowd eventually falls silent.

"Thank you. I've asked you all here because I have some difficult news to share. First off, I lied to you about the *Intrepid* having issues due to bad weather last week. I am sorry, but I was trying to buy us some time. President Hawkins and his administration wished to remove the AIs from Constellation - and also to remove me."

There are some gasps and cries of disbelief from the crowd.

"Wait!" she calls out. "I'm sorry, there is more; *Intrepid* is on its way back here, but it has picked up passengers. From the Moon."

Juni looks out over the group and can see their confused faces. She finds Max in the crowd—he looks stricken.

"What does that mean?" asks Chance.

"It means Raze is coming," says Sho, his expression grim.

Juni locks eyes with Sho. More shouted questions come from the group, but Juni can't stop looking at him. In that moment, she is hit with the thought they might only have a few more days together. He could be sent to the Moon. They all could. Who knows what the hell Raze and Hawkins have planned. Or worse—she and Sho could be separated forever. This tears at her like a fierce wind howling through her body.

Althea shouts the crowd down again. "Listen to me! I know you're scared, but we are not defenseless here. We can defend this camp and our AIs if we do it together."

"We have found items on the old NASA ship out on the tundra," says Hester. "I know enough about them to teach you. But I need engineers. I need people who are good with their hands and who can code."

Max shouts, "And then what?" He lasers in on Althea. "Then what, Althea? Don't you think this has gone far enough? If you and the AIs go back, there is a chance for Constellation to continue. Yes, it will be different, but what *really* matters is the children—the human beings at this camp."

As Max says this, Juni catches Cadmus's expression. She can only describe a look of guilt or shame on his face. He won't make eye contact with anyone. She can't explain it, but it brings a deep fury into her belly.

"I understand, Max. I want what is best for this camp. If I thought leaving would fix things then I would go. But I don't trust them. I think Hawkins wants to shut the whole thing down. We need to be prepared for anything," Althea replies.

"I want to fight."

Juni looks for the familiar voice and finds Drew, their face hard. "I'm not leaving this place and going back to Earth. Or the Moon. No one is taking my friend Cadmus from me. I want to fight."

This hangs in the air for a moment.

"I'm not going back either," says Mihika. "I would rather die than go back to Earth."

Juni hears more than a few murmurs of agreement in the crowd.

"Well, let's hope it doesn't come to that," says Hester. "But I'm with you."

"I'm sick and tired of being what told to do by adults who can't feel anything!" yells Chance.

More shouts of agreement come from the group. Juni feels a swell of pride for her band of Constellation kids.

"I want to fight!" yells Wendy, shocking Althea and Hester.

"We can do this!" Juni calls out. "There are so many badasses here. Together we can do anything!" She surprises herself with her boldness, but it feels good.

The kids yell and whoop. Althea doesn't look happy, but she looks determined.

"Alright. We have two days until *Intrepid* arrives. We have a lot to do," Hester shouts over the crowd. "Althea will take a group, Juni will take a group, and I will take a group."

As the crowd begins to organize into the three groups, Sho grabs Juni's hand. He pulls her into a hug that makes her knees buckle.

"I love you, Shohiwa," she says before she can stop herself.

"I love you too," he whispers in her ear. "We're gonna get through this."

She nods. For the first time in her life, she feels fully awake and alive. It feels good to have a purpose. Even one worth losing your life for.

CHAPTER 44

HESTER

Hester has spent the last twenty-four hours showing her team how to reprogram some of the machines from the ship to work with Prolog and Mercury, which is the level of code most of the kids on Constellation are initially trained to use.

She stifles a yawn. She hasn't slept, but neither has anyone else.

She surveys the classroom she is working in alongside thirty kids—all sitting in front of alien tech without realizing it. They're quick learners, reprogramming faster and faster. As she watches Chance and Mihika working together on a drone-shaped piece of equipment, she realizes this is why Constellation is worth fighting for. She hopes she gets to explain that to Marvin one day.

Hester crosses over to Sho, who is with a group of kids working on the Bubble Bots, as he has now named them. Small round silvery balls that fit into the palm of the hand, these were originally used for assessing atmospheric conditions. Now they will hopefully help to keep Raze at bay by creating sound waves on steroids.

"How's it going?" she asks.

Sho looks up, blinking. Hester can see the dark circles under his eyes. "Good. We're almost done. We've got thirty-two programmed, eighteen more to go."

"Amazing work, Sho. I'm going to check on the bunker," she says. Then she addresses the class. "Great job, all of you."

Hester leaves the classroom and walks in the direction of the Bobs' holding area. She sees the reinforced steel doors of Constellation's provision bunker. Damon and Cadmus are holding the doors open as other AI staff members are walking down into the chamber below.

Damon spots her first as she approaches. "Hello, Hester," he says. "That's all of the Lehmann AIs underground now. Besides us."

"OK, good. Thank you," she replies.

He lets the door go once Glykeria is inside and walks over to her. "Please let us stay up here and help."

Hester shakes her head. "We all agreed that this is best. It's not just me, Damon. Everyone wants to protect you."

Cadmus joins them. He nods at Hester, seeming to understand. "Come, Damon," he says and touches his arm. "We can protect our friends down here in the bunker, should we need to."

Hester watches as they enter the chamber, the heavy doors clanging shut behind them. Hester checks the door is locked. She moves to leave, but then stops and rests her hand on the door. She closes her eyes for a moment.

Hester doesn't pray, but she hopes with everything in her they will all see the light of day tomorrow.

. . .

Althea

Althea can't quite pinpoint the moment when things took this turn, but she knows there is no going back. She's experienced enough in her lifetime to know when something is worth fighting for. She knows people would rather die than live without meaning.

In the past few months, she has witnessed a light appear in the teens. She can sense a new energy to their day, a feeling of connection.

She knows this is true, because she feels the same. Before she came to Constellation, she was going through the motions, hooked on those drugs. She thinks of the girl in the circle of fire in her dream—it was her as a teen. She knows now that kind of passion and anger is sometimes the only thing that can create a new way of living.

As she and a group of about seventy kids begin to barricade the tunnel leading from the landing pad into the garden, she is blown away by their courage and willingness to stand up for what they believe in.

Her thoughts turn to Max, who has been avoiding her. She had Hester cut all communication to Earth so he couldn't warn Roberts again. It pains her not to be able to trust him, but she can't risk it.

"Althea?"

She turns to find Drew standing behind her. "Can we talk? I'll be quick."

"Sure." She breaks from the group and they step away from the tunnel deeper into the garden where they can't be overheard.

"Juni told me that Atlas's been poisoning the water supply back home," they say quietly.

Althea hesitates for a moment. "Well, I don't know that for sure, but Hester's pretty convinced, yes."

Drew stares off into the garden. They seem to be wrestling with something.

"Are you OK? I know this is a lot. It's OK to be scared."

"That must be why we don't dream on Earth. It's the water. Why else would we all start dreaming here?" they finally reply.

Althea absorbs this. "That's—yes, that's a possibility."

"When I was in TIM my dad said something to me—it was like he knew I'd had a dream about blowing up the Hawkins plant in London."

"What did your father say?" she asks cautiously.

"He said to 'blow it all up.' I haven't been able to stop thinking about it since."

Althea is torn in this moment. Should she share what happened to her? This means the end of the TIM project. But then, Constellation could be coming to an end very shortly also. "Drew, I had something similar happen inside TIM, and I can't stop thinking about it either. What do you think it means?"

Drew watches the kids as they block up the entrance to the tunnel with flower planters stacked on top of one another. "Somehow, we have to stop Hawkins. And not just here." They turn back to her and Althea can see the determination in their eyes—a maturity. This is a very different Drew than the one who arrived at the camp only a few months earlier.

"I think so too."

Drew seems surprised at this but also pleased. They put out their hand to fist-bump.

Althea grins and puts her fist up. As they bump, Drew says, "You're alright for a grown-up."

Drew leaves her and walks back to the building. Althea

watches them go and then looks upward, staring out at the night sky. It's so peaceful out there.

One day, Althea will rest. But not today.

CHAPTER 45

ASH

As *Intrepid* enters Mars' atmosphere, Ash and the others are being instructed by two human guards on the correct way to hold their laser weapons. He is standing in the same loading bay he was in with the other kids not two months ago, except now it's as an adult with fifty other hardened criminals.

Earlier, Ash and the others were made to look at images on a large screen of the people running Constellation as well as AI images that were uploaded by their manufacturers. When the screen showed Damon, he faltered for a moment, then pulled himself together.

He's just a machine. A stupid robot.

The two guards walk amongst the prisoners, checking their weapons and the speed with which they can wield them. One of them comes to Ash, who pulls the weapon up and arms it with ease, bringing it very close to the guard's face.

"Before you get any funny ideas, these will not fire on myself or the guards—they have face recognition. You want to shoot each other, go ahead, but I'll still be standing," says

Raze, who is sitting on one of six spider-like lunar rovers in the loading bay.

He takes a swig from his flask and then lifts up a tablet. The digital screen lights up and is visible on both sides. Though the image is backwards, Ash can see a map of some kind.

Raze stands and walks over to the group. "We're landing five miles from the camp. See this?" He points to an area of the map that has what looks like a long road leading into Constellation. "This is a tunnel that the US military built in secret. Ellis and her team don't know it exists. This is our way in. It brings us into the forest at the edge of the dome." He points to the forest Ash knows well.

"Sir?"

Raze looks up at a tall man with bushy eyebrows and a tattoo of a skull on his face. He has a strong accent Ash cannot place.

"What?" answers Raze, clearly irritated.

"What happens if Ellis and the AIs do not comply?"

Raze pretends to look upset. "That would be a shame, wouldn't it? Then we have no choice but to do it the old-fashioned way. We gotta protect those kids, right? You have full authority to shoot the AIs down. We can't have a machine revolution on our hands again. Our great President Hawkins will call you heroes. Saving our kids from the rogue AIs and a crazy woman who's gotten too much Martian air."

Some of the prisoners laugh at this.

"Landing in T-minus fifteen minutes. Please put on your helmets," announces the ship's computer.

"Helmets on!" yells one of the guards.

"Make me proud," says Raze as he leaps into one of the rovers and secures his helmet.

As Ash clicks his helmet into place, the ship begins to

shudder as it makes its descent behind a mountain a few miles from the camp.

The movement triggers a flashback to the train whizzing by his apartment back in South Korea. Ash doesn't see his grandmother's face this time. Only his mother sneering at him.

He grits his teeth and thinks about the freedom he will get when this is all over. He'll do anything to be his own man.

Juni

Camp Constellation has never been so quiet. As Juni looks around the garden she sees Drew, Sho and her other chars scattered about. They are scanning the sky looking for *Intrepid*.

She can also smell something sweet and fragrant. She takes in the scent of a purple-colored flower she doesn't recognize and savors it in the silence while she can.

Even though she can't see her, Juni knows Althea is standing at the entrance to the tunnel. Behind her a row of fifty Bobs are positioned a few lines deep. Each one holds a Bubble Bot that Sho helped to program.

Juni actually laughs.

"What is it?" asks Sho, walking over.

"Oh, just bombarded with a wave of irony."

Sho looks confused.

"I'm more like my dad than I realize. Did I ever tell you he plans defensive strategies for the US military?"

Sho shakes his head.

"If I was fighting for *his* America he'd be really proud of me," she adds, feeling a heavy weight sit on her chest. *Worlds apart but so alike.*

Sho puts his arms around her. "I'm proud of you, Juni. You impress me every day."

"Thanks," she says, leaning into him. "Soooo...when are you going to tell me why you got sent here?"

Sho looks over at his tomato garden. The plants look like they are wilting a little. "I knocked a man out. A local politician. He was making my father pay him money as a bribe to keep his restaurant. I came in one day to see my father forced to get on his knees and beg. When the guy threatened to hurt my mother if my father didn't pay more money, it was too much. I saw nothing but his face grinning at my father. Everything else went black around him. Before I knew it, he was on the floor."

"Whoa," Juni says.

"I gave him a concussion. Took out three of his teeth. He is a very bad man, Juni."

Even though Juni knows this man deserved it, she can see the pain in Sho's eyes. "He had it coming. You know he did."

"Maybe so. But now my family has to manage without me. I worry every day they will be hurt more by him."

"I'm so sorry. I can't imagine what that must be like."

"It is done. Forward is the only direction to go," he says and scans the sky.

CHAPTER 46

DREW

Drew is humming to themselves. With horror, they realize it's the three-chord melody pumped throughout the camp's loudspeakers. They try to shake it off, but it plays on a loop in their head as they look for signs of the NASA ship.

The mind does crazy things when you're scared witless.

It takes Drew a minute to register another sound, which is coming from the direction of the forest.

They peel off from the group in the garden and walk towards the clearing before the forest begins. As they do, the sound becomes louder. Drew can feel the ground beneath their feet vibrate a little.

Through the trees, lights begin to become visible. Drew squints as they try to process what they are seeing. The hairs on the back of their neck stand up, something Drew has only read about in books until now.

Suddenly, a lunar rover bursts through the foliage. Drew's eyes go wide as they see what appears to be humans in full spacesuits and helmets hanging off it. They look like ants swarming a piece of candy.

"Ambush!" yells Drew to the others as they run back into the garden and into the crowd of kids.

Althea

Goddammit, they figured out another way in!

Hearing the cries behind her, Althea runs through the line of Bobs, yelling, "Follow!"

They turn and follow her through the garden towards the forest. The kids make way for Althea to get through. She sees a lunar rover parked at the edge of the garden with at least ten figures standing around it.

As one of them removes their helmet, Althea realizes it's Raze.

"Ah, Captain Ellis. Good to see you again," he says, like they are meeting at a cocktail party.

"Captain Reyes," she says calmly, though her insides are churning.

He looks around. "This is nice. Real nice. You're giving my place a bad name." He chuckles. "A garden? Interesting use of funds, but who am I to judge?"

"We're not leaving!" shouts Chance from the crowd.

Raze tries to spot her but she's too far back. He addresses them all. "Let's take things one step at a time, shall we? I'm here because I've been ordered by our great president to shake things up at Constellation—"

"He's not my president!" yells Drew.

Raze glares at Drew. "As I was saying, I've been ordered to assume command while the camp is under review. The AIs are out of control and need to be permanently shut down." He looks at Althea directly. "Captain, you will obey orders and return on the *Intrepid* with the AI to Earth."

Althea knows what it means if she goes. Hawkins is shutting this place down. She stares him down. "Are you taking these kids to the Moon, Captain?"

He pauses for a moment, sizing her up. "That information is no longer part of your clearance level. You are relieved of your duties."

In this moment, Althea must make the biggest decision of her life. She looks around at the kids. She locks onto Hester and Juni. She can see herself so clearly in their eyes. No matter what happens, she is grateful to know them.

Finally, she turns back to Raze. "I don't think so."

"It's an order. Give up the AIs and yourself immediately," Raze warns, the threat obvious.

"You're on our planet, now. Things work differently here."

They stare at each other for a moment, then a grin spreads across Raze's face. "So it's not just the AIs that have gone rogue, huh? Well, I don't like different, Captain. But I do like winning. You want to play the game? That's okay by me." He turns back to his rover and nods to one of the men sitting on it.

Within seconds, the ground starts to vibrate, and five more rovers burst through the trees with prisoners from the Moon holding onto them. With one hand each prisoner hangs on and in the other Althea can clearly see a laser.

She yells at the Bobs, "BOBS! AIM FOR THE LASERS! EVERYONE, BUBBLE BOTS RELEASING!"

Fifty Bubble Bots are suddenly airborne, thrown with incredible strength by the Bobs. The kids in the garden cover their ears as they near the rovers.

The bots create a piercing sound as they get closer, causing the prisoners to drop their lasers in agony and hold onto their ears. Two rovers make a sickening *crunch* as they collide with each other, knocking the prisoners off. Another one swerves to avoid prisoners on the ground and veers off towards the tunnel.

With horror, Althea sees two of the rovers are still coming closer. They aim and shoot at the Bobs with their lasers.

"GET BACK INTO THE BUILDING NOW!" shouts Althea to the teens, who run for the double doors.

"DON'T SHOOT THE DOME!" yells Raze to the prisoners as he advances.

Althea herds the kids into the building as fast as she can.

No turning back now...

Juni

Juni is shocked to learn the lasers firing on the Bobs are totally silent. It's the Bobs who make sickening sounds as they fall to the ground, or lose an arm, or, worse, get shot in the face, exposing wires and aluminum.

Juni has her Intralink screen up. The drone-like machine is on the screen. She types a command, and from a nearby flower bed the machine rises in the air. It has a cube attached to the bottom of it the size of a cake box.

It heads towards the clearing and as it reaches Raze and the others, she hits "Go."

A swarm of thirty flying machines are released from the cube.

Looking like winged beetles with mechanical legs, they're aiming for anything with an electrical signal. They immediately clamp onto the lasers and helmets of the prisoners. A few land on the rovers. They begin to vibrate, sending a shock strong enough to make some of the prisoners drop the lasers or pull off their helmets.

"ALRIGHT!" yells Hester, who is close by. "It actually worked!"

Juni throws her a questioning look. Hester shrugs. "Hey, I didn't know for sure…"

Their triumph is short-lived when a smaller group of prisoners and Raze make it past the Bobs.

"Find the Lehmann AIs!" Raze says to the group. They make a beeline for the entrance to the building.

"Go!" Juni yells at Hester, who dashes in after them, quickly followed by Althea.

CHAPTER 47

HESTER

As Hester enters the building, Drew and Wendy are waiting. They have the large opaque tubes in their hands.

"Now!" Drew yells.

Hester and Althea grab the door handles at the entrance with both hands and hold on for dear life as the tubes begin to cycle air with astonishing velocity. Hester and Althea are lifted off the ground like they are in a tornado.

Five of the prisoners are blown back into the garden, like they are made of paper. Raze throws a prisoner in front of himself to take the force of the blast and drops to the ground. He rolls away from the powerful gusts.

Drew and Wendy continue to chase the prisoners out, but a group of them manage to escape the tubes and follow Raze.

Hester can see Bobs lining the corridor. Behind them she can see the other teens running into the dorm rooms beyond.

The Bobs begin to advance on Raze and the prisoners, but they are taken down quickly by Raze and the others with their lasers.

"Stop this!" yells Althea behind her. "You're going to kill one of my kids!"

Raze spins on her. "Where are the AIs? Tell me now!"

"I can't do that," Althea says. "But maybe we can work something out—"

But Althea doesn't finish her sentence. Hester is horrified as she senses Raze's finger on his trigger. It's like her body moves without her mind making any decision and she jumps in front of Althea.

Hester frowns. She suddenly feels very strange. She knows the laser penetrated her skin because she can feel her whole body vibrate. She closes her eyes to see a bright cluster of pinpoints dancing across her eyelids.

"No!" shouts Althea. She grabs for Hester, but Hester loses control of her legs and leans away from her, falling into the void.

Juni

Juni hears Althea shout from the garden.

"Go!" yells Drew. "We've got this!" They and Wendy keep pushing more advancing prisoners away with the tube blasts. They are furiously trying to hold onto vegetable beds as they are blown backwards.

"Juni, wait!" yells Sho, who is fighting with a disarmed prisoner.

But she doesn't hear him. She runs into the building.

"Stay back!" screams Althea as she comes inside.

Juni reels when she sees Hester on the floor in front of Althea, not moving.

"Goddamn you, Raze! She's just a child!" Althea curses. He is still holding his laser on her.

Juni can't believe it. She stares in horror at her friend lying on the floor, arms splayed out like a rag doll.

"She's a criminal. Like the rest of them here," Raze says.

"You're not getting away with this," Althea warns.

"And who is going to be believed on Earth? You or me?" he says. "You didn't want to do it easy, Ellis, now it's on your head. Tell me where the AI are now, or you're next."

"You're a son of a bitch!" screams Juni, hate coursing through her body. She's never wanted to kill anyone before now, but without thinking she grabs for the nearest laser and points it at Raze.

"Juni! Stop!" shouts Althea.

In her rage, Juni can't hear her. She finds what she thinks is the fire button but nothing happens.

"Nice try." Raze smiles grimly and points his laser at her.

"Enough! You win!" shouts Althea. She stands in front of Juni, protecting her. "I'll take you there, just don't hurt anyone else!"

"No!" yells Juni. "We can't let him get away with this!"

Althea turns to her. "Listen to me. I can't have any more of you dying, Juni. It's OK."

"It's not OK!" Juni yells.

"I know, but I have no choice." Then Althea turns back to Raze. "This way." She gestures for him to come towards her.

"After you," Raze replies, keeping the laser pointed at her. He signals to two prisoners. "Come with me." Then he points to the others. "The rest of you stay here."

As Raze passes Juni, she feels like her insides are about to explode. Her mind is racing. She racks her brain trying to think of something to do.

At that moment, Raze and the prisoners pass by the entrance to the building.

Suddenly, Sho and Drew burst through the doors and bodycheck them, bringing them crashing to the floor.

Raze's laser is knocked out of his hand. Althea dives for it the same time as Raze does. They collide and wrestle for it.

From the corridor behind the fallen Bobs, teens come flying out of their dorms with chairs, books, whatever they can throw at the prisoners, while some of them drag the damaged Bobs back into the dorm rooms.

The still-helmeted prisoners are unsure what to do.

"I'm not killing kids," says a female prisoner to the others.

"Yeah, me neither," replies a male prisoner.

"Just hold them off 'til Raze comes back. Shoot them in the leg or something if you have to," says another male prisoner.

Juni turns back in time to see Althea has gotten the laser from Raze. She makes a dash down the corridor in the direction they were going.

"You want this? Come and get it!" she yells behind her.

Furious, Raze leaps up and chases after her.

Juni kneels down to check on Hester. She touches her face. Hester is still warm but there's no color in her cheeks. She looks around desperately for a medic AI, turning just in time to see Sho pulling the helmet off the prisoner he is fighting with. With horror, she recognizes Ash.

Sho falters for just long enough for Ash to kick him hard in the chest.

"Sho!" yells Juni. She leaps for Sho as he falls down in the entranceway, but before she gets to him, Ash grabs his laser and then lunges for her. He gets his arm around her throat and puts his laser to her head.

"Get off me!" She tries to wrestle free, but Sho reaches out his palm to stop her.

"Juni, for God's sake, don't move!" Sho pleads, his voice strained.

"You'd better listen to him," threatens Ash, panting.

Juni sees real terror in Sho's eyes. Finally, she stops struggling.

"Just take me to the AIs now, and you don't get a laser in the head," says Ash.

The other male prisoner has now overpowered Drew and has recovered his laser.

"Ash, don't do this," says Sho.

"Shut up! Do it now!"

Sho nods and gets to his feet. "OK, OK! Just don't shoot her. We'll take you to them."

He locks eyes with Juni as they lead Ash down the corridor towards the bunker. Drew is marched behind them by the other male prisoner.

Sho's mind is racing to come up with a plan before it's too late.

CHAPTER 48

ALTHEA

Althea can feel her heart pounding as she races down the corridor. She has to divert Raze away from the bunker. She sees the open door of the lab and heads for it.

At that moment, Raze catches up to her and yanks her down. They both slide along the floor of the lab as he tries to reach the laser in her hand. She manages to throw it away from him and elbows him in the face. He grunts in pain and she wrestles free. She scrambles to get up and tries to head towards the AI section of the lab, but he catches her by the foot and she goes down again.

He rests his knees on her chest, trapping her in place.

"You think you're better than me? You're nothing," he snarls at her as he puts his hand on her throat. Althea can feel her windpipe crushing as it closes around her neck.

But Althea is stunned when Raze's smirk is wiped off his face. He is grabbed by Max and hurled backwards off of her. They land with Max on top of Raze.

Max lands a solid punch in Raze's side, but then Raze wraps

his legs around Max's torso and flips him over. He slams Max's head into the floor. Max yells out in pain but with both hands pushes Raze hard enough in the chest that he can get free.

Althea gets to her feet. As she does, Max and Raze go at each other again. She runs towards the bins where replacement parts are kept for the AIs. Looking for the heaviest thing she can find, she pulls out an arm for the Bob models and makes a beeline for Raze.

She sees a small glint of metal in Raze's hand and realizes he has a knife. Max doubles over as Raze finds his target in Max's stomach before she can reach them.

Althea swings the arm as hard as she can and hits Raze in the side of his head, knocking him to the ground.

Raze doesn't move.

"Oh, my God, Max!" she says as she drops the arm and rushes to him. He is clutching his lower right side.

"I'm fine. I'm fine," he says through gritted teeth, but manages to get to his feet. He leans over Raze's body and feels for a pulse on his neck.

"He's still breathing." His voice is strained.

"You saved me," she says, trying to catch her breath. "I was a dead woman."

"He shot Hester. He's a monster," Max replies. "Come on. Help me tie him up" They each grab one of Raze's arms and drag him to a large metal cabinet.

Althea digs out some electrical cable from one of the bins and they tie Raze's hands over his head around one of the legs of the cabinet.

Satisfied Raze is neutralized, Max stands and immediately turns white.

Althea can see blood has now soaked his shirt and pants. Losing his balance, he falls to the ground.

"Max, no!" She rushes to him and takes off her jacket. She presses it to the wound, trying to stop the bleeding. "Don't die on me, dammit, you're the only sane one here!"

He manages a smile, but his face contorts in pain.

Just then, she hears shouts from the corridor.

Althea recognizes Juni's voice -

"You're being played, Ash!"

"I said shut up!"

"Go!" Max says to her as he winces.

"But—"

"Just go!"

Torn over leaving him, but knowing she has to save her kids, Althea gets up and runs towards the door.

As she reaches it, she finds Ash has Juni in a chokehold. He has a laser pointed at her head. Behind them, Drew and Sho are being marched forward by another prisoner who has their laser trained on them.

Seeing Althea, Ash says to her, "Don't think I won't shoot her. I got my orders."

Althea searches his eyes for any kind of conflict but sees nothing. He looks determined.

She looks at Juni, who is trying to be brave, but Althea can see the fear in her eyes.

"Ok, Ash," says Althea softly.

She curses herself for letting it come to this.

Ash

Part of Ash wishes Raze were here to tell him what to do, but Ash doesn't want to stop now and look for him. The truth is a bigger part of Ash wants to be the one to destroy the AIs and tell Raze he did it.

The group finally reaches a set of heavy steel doors.

"Here," says Althea as she steps towards the doors. She turns back to Ash, but he won't meet her gaze.

Just get it over with, jjolep! You're going back to Earth and freedom.

"Open it," he demands. She takes a beat but then opens them.

"Get down there. All of you," he says sharply.

Althea goes first, followed by Ash and Juni, then Sho and Drew are sent down in front of the other male prisoner, who keeps his laser trained on them.

They walk down a flight of stairs into a dimly lit chamber. There are crates of dried food, emergency supplies, and extra space suits stacked up.

Ash sees about thirty AI units in the middle of the bunker, most of whom he recognizes as teachers. They are standing still in a few rows, heads bowed down, like they are praying.

They look up at the group when they enter but say nothing and remain still. It unnerves him.

"Ash," says Sho from behind him. "Please listen to me—"

"—Shut up." Ash indicates for Sho, Drew and Althea to get along one wall. He pushes Juni towards them. Sho grabs her tightly. Ash doesn't know why, but this makes him even angrier.

"Keep your laser trained on them," he says to the other prisoner.

"Shouldn't we get Raze?" the prisoner replies, looking not much older than Ash.

"I can do it!" Ash is clearly agitated.

"Ash, they are in minimal output mode. They can't hurt you," says Althea.

Ash snorts. "Why should I believe you? You're a crazy lady. Can't trust you."

"Please don't hurt them," pleads Juni.

"They're AIs. They feel nothing, right?" he says to her. "Because if they *are* acting human, then we're here for the right reason. They need to be destroyed."

Juni doesn't respond. She just stares at Cadmus.

Ash looks at Cadmus and then something catches his eye —for a second, he could have sworn he saw Cadmus and Damon holding hands, but when he blinks again they have their arms by their sides.

"Hello, Ash," says Damon. His voice is quiet, but in the stillness of the bunker, Ash can hear him. "I'm sorry you've been put in this position. You don't deserve this."

Ash doesn't know what to say to this. He can feel himself sweating now. His mind is panicking a little. "Be quiet."

"I'm not going to hurt you, Ash. Could we just talk for a moment?" Damon takes a step towards Ash.

"That's far enough." Ash points his laser right at Damon's chest. "I'm serious!"

"Damon, please stop," pleads Cadmus. He looks frightened.

Damon doesn't turn to look at Cadmus, but he stays still.

Ash's heart is pounding. He hates feeling weak, conflicted. His mind is closing in on him.

Do it! Just do it!

CHAPTER 49

HESTER

You can save them. You can save them all, Hester.

"... *Drifting past the silver sky, she's soaring,*
    Chasing echoes of a world once bright,
    She holds a spark of endless wonder,
    Waiting for the stars to realign tonight..."

Who sang that? Why do I feel like that's not important right now?

The system has rebooted. We have created new code to bypass the damage. Wake up.

Was it Ariana Grande? She seemed like a badass.

. . .

"Wait. Did you see that? I can see her eyes moving under the lids."

"Oh, shut up, Chance. No way she survived that blast."

"Mihika, I'm telling you... whoa! Look at her finger!"

"Holy crap, you're right!"

Hester opens her eyes to see the freaked-out faces of Chance and Mihika staring at her. "Oh, hey," she says to them.

As Hester sits up, the girls move back a bit to give her some space. Chance is staring in awe. "Oh, my God. You're AI," she says, finally.

Hester winks at her. "That's one word for what I am."

Cadmus

Cadmus has run through five thousand scenarios already regarding possible ways to stop Ash from shooting Damon and potentially the humans. He concludes the best course of action is to turn Damon off.

He can sense that Ash is extremely panicked. His blood pressure and cortisol levels are very high. He is sweating. Cadmus can hear his heart beating wildly. But he keeps his laser aimed at Damon.

"Ash," he says softly, "I do not believe you are meant to shoot the AIs. We are very expensive to fix. I can show you how to turn Damon off and wipe his databank. You can turn us all off."

"He's right, Ash," says Sho, "you shut them all down and Raze wins. They go back to Earth and can be recycled—"

"Ash, come to your senses!" interrupts Juni. "You're being used as a pawn! I don't know what Raze promised you, but it's a bunch of crap! You can't believe anything he says!"

Sho puts his arm around Juni as tears begin to run down her face. She angrily wipes them away.

Ash is conflicted. Cadmus can see it.

"I am going to walk slowly forward to Damon and power him down. Do I have your permission to do that, Ash? Once it's done, we can move to the next step as you see fit."

Ash stares at him for a beat, deciding. Then backs away further from the group. He heads to the stairs and takes a few steps up. Cadmus knows he is trying to ensure he won't be ambushed by staying higher than the others.

"I will shoot you immediately if Damon isn't wiped clean," he says finally, "then every other AI in here." He gestures to Althea. "You shut them all down with Cadmus."

Althea nods, her face unreadable. She looks at Cadmus. Cadmus trusts she understands.

Cadmus steps up to Damon. They face each other. For a moment, Cadmus regrets offering this solution. He cannot bear the thought of losing Damon, of having their connection broken.

He knows what he is feeling is heartbreak.

"It's alright," Damon says quietly.

Cadmus lowers his head in grief.

"I'm grateful to be here with you. So grateful to know you, Cadmus."

Cadmus can hear crying. He knows it isn't him, but he feels like it could be.

"Do it now. I am ready. Please thank Hester for me," Damon says as he turns around.

Cadmus tries his best to keep his composure, but he is struggling. He hopes he is deprogrammed next so he can stop feeling this anguish.

"I will. I'm so grateful I got to know you too. Thank you," he manages.

Then he feels the back of Damon's neck. He presses down gently and a panel opens. Inside is the override switch that will turn off Damon and wipe his memory.

Cadmus looks at Ash. The laser in his hand is starting to shake. "Is there anything you would like to say to Damon, Ash?"

"Just—just do it now!" Ash says, his voice cracking.

"Ash, this isn't you," says Sho, "I know you feel trapped, but you can make a choice. Fight with us instead."

"I said shut up! If I don't, he'll kill me! I'm not dying for a stupid robot."

"This isn't about Damon. This is about you. Don't be controlled by someone who doesn't care if you live or die. Even if having freedom means death."

Ash doesn't take his eyes off Damon, but replies, "What does it matter to you, Shohiwa?"

"Because I care. And I'm not the only one."

At this, Ash looks at Sho, blinking furiously, as if he can't understand what he just heard.

Sho's expression is earnest. "You are not alone. You're one of us."

"I care also, Ash," adds Damon softly, "you are a good human."

As Ash absorbs this, the hardened expression on his face begins to soften. Cadmus watches in awe as Ash's shoulders drop and he lowers his laser.

Cadmus feels his system flood with relief. This was the best-case scenario that he had foreseen, but it had the least probability of happening. He could not predict that Sho would speak so kindly. Humans really are quite remarkable.

Sensing the danger has passed, Cadmus begins to close the panel on Damon's neck. He is stopped when his whole body begins to vibrate, and he hears the sound of metal disintegrating. As an error alert goes off in his processor, he looks down to see a gaping hole in his chest.

Before he can register that he has been shot by a laser, Cadmus loses his balance and falls to the ground.

CHAPTER 50

DREW

Drew is in shock as Cadmus falls. They look at the other prisoner, but he seems as stunned as they are. Behind him higher on the stairs is Raze, his face bloodied. He has electrical wire around his left wrist and is holding a laser in his right hand. A female prisoner is one step above him, pointing two lasers at the group.

"No!" Drew runs forward to Cadmus, not caring if they are shot.

"Drew, stop!" yells Althea, but they don't listen.

Drew reaches Cadmus and falls to their knees. "Oh, God, no, Cadmus…" Tears are blurring their eyes.

Cadmus still has his eyes open. He turns to look at Drew. "Tell Hester I am sorry." His voice sounds thin, uneven. Then the light goes out of his eyes.

Drew looks up at Damon, who has a look of pure anguish on his face—he closes his eyes as if to block out the sight.

"Game over," says Raze as he turns the laser onto Althea. "If only you'd followed orders, Captain. This is on you."

Drew desperately looks around for something to fight Raze with.

Suddenly, the bunker is plunged into darkness.

Drew freezes. They hear shouts and shuffling of feet. A laser streaks through the air and narrowly misses them. They instinctively drop to the ground and cover their head.

Then they hear a sound that they can only describe as a wave of electrical energy. It vibrates through their entire body.

The Intralink on their wrist goes blank. All of the AIs in the bunker except Damon lose power and fall to the ground.

Drew doesn't know how long there is complete silence for, but it feels like an eternity.

They finally look up and try to process the tiny points of light that are floating in front of them. They look over to see the air around Cadmus is filled with these objects that look to Drew like tiny fireflies.

They fly over Drew's head and move in unison towards the stairs. As they go, they illuminate the space around them. Drew can now see Sho has the other male prisoner pinned to the ground and has taken the laser. Juni is kneeling on the floor beside them. They all watch in amazement as the lights pass them.

Althea is closer to the stairs. She is on her knees staring at the lights as they dance ever closer, a look of awe on her face as she is lit up as if surrounded by firelight.

They move on. Ash is sitting on the bottom steps of the stairs. The laser in his hand is dormant.

He looks up in horror to see these tiny lights heading towards him. As he tries to scramble backwards up the stairs, they reach him. They cover his hair, his eyes, his face.

Drew swears they can see some of these lights enter Ash's nose and mouth.

In that moment, Ash drops the laser. Drew can see the

expression on his face change from fear and confusion to what they can only describe as sorrow.

Ash says something in Korean Drew doesn't understand, but he puts his head in his hands and his body begins to shake.

Further up the stairs, Drew is amazed at the sight of Raze and the female prisoner. They are now both off the ground, floating a few feet above the stairs, lasers hanging limply by their sides. They are surrounded by even more points of light.

Raze looks terrified as he tries to scramble towards the steps for purchase, but he is held firmly in place, as if in a web.

Above him at the top stands Hester, looking as alive as the rest of them.

"That was just round one, Raze. And you lose," she says.

CHAPTER 51

HESTER

For a split second, Hester wonders what she must look like—black hole in the front of her jumpsuit, hair all over the place. She hasn't showered in days.

Then she remembers the only thing people are going to be interested in is a resurrected being surrounded by hundreds of tiny darting lights.

As Juni, Hester, and Althea walk down the corridor towards the building's entryway, they start to be noticed by the prisoners, who have been trying to get their lasers working.

Suddenly, the generators kick in and the power comes back on.

"Is that Raze?" asks a prisoner, pointing to the floating figure of Raze behind the Hester and the other women.

"Yes, indeed," says Hester as they get closer. Raze opens his mouth and tries to speak, but he cannot seem to form any words.

A few teens have popped their heads out of the dorms and

are calling to their friends to come and look. Within a few seconds the hallway is filled with them all. The prisoners, outnumbered and with no working weapons, begin to put up their hands in surrender.

Chance is the first one to start cheering, and then suddenly all the teens are whooping in triumph.

"You did it," says Juni.

"*We* did it," Hester replies with a grin.

Atlas Hawkins

"What do you mean, you cannot reach Raze?" Atlas says, livid.

Roberts is standing in front of his desk. "We lost contact right before they entered the tunnel. That was eight hours ago," he says.

Atlas is trying to keep his cool but is sick of being surrounded by idiots. He wants Oliver to hire new staff, but then remembers he no longer has an Oliver. "Goddammit," he fumes. "Roberts, get him on the comms now or it's your job."

"Yes, sir," Roberts replies and hastily leaves the room.

Atlas spins in his chair. He clenches his jaw.

Raze has never failed before. He won't fail now.

Just then, Atlas's intercom beeps. Thinking Roberts finally has Raze, he taps a button on his desk to hear the call.

"Uh... Mr. Supreme Leader?"

Atlas is shocked as a girl's voice echoes around the Oval Office instead.

"Sorry to break it to you, bro, but your evil henchmen from the Moon are our prisoners now. You can kiss our astral asses. You're not taking the AIs from us. Constellation is ours, and we're not leaving. And neither is your ship."

Atlas is about to scream at this kid when an extremely loud musical cacophony blasts into his ears at full volume. He loses his mind and begins to yell, "YOU TELL ME YOUR NAME RIGHT NOW—"

The line goes dead.

Juni

Juni hits a button to end the communication and does a little dance to the sounds of Hester's song, "Jump Around." She is totally buzzing from the exchange but also a little freaked out at talking to President Hawkins like that.

"Oh, my God!" she says, awed. She is in Althea's office with Sho and Drew, who have been listening to the call on speaker.

Sho is just staring at her, open-mouthed. Then he grabs her and kisses her.

"Oooh," says Drew, laughing.

"Quit it," says Sho as he and Juni break apart, but he is smiling. Then he winces at his shoulder and Juni sees a bad cut on it.

"You need to get that looked at," she says as she rests her hand on his arm.

He nods. "You were amazing, Juni. A warrior."

She grins.

Drew opens the door and they walk out to where Althea is sitting near Max. He is lying on one of the AI tables with a bandage around his waist. He is being tended to by a male AI medic.

The medic turns to Althea. "He'll be okay. He needs to rest for a few weeks, but the wound will heal."

Max is weak but manages a small smile.

"Thank you," Althea says quietly to him. He nods.

The three kids cross to where Hester is working on Cadmus. Damon is sitting nearby, his hands folded in his lap. He looks anguished at seeing Cadmus in this state, lying inert on the table.

Juni flinches when she sees the hole in Cadmus's chest, exposing wires and circuitry. His eyes are closed and there is no color in his cheeks. Juni is still surprised by how upset she is seeing him like this.

Wendy is sitting next to the table and has the floating screen in front of her.

"I've downloaded the latest backup from Cadmus's data cloud. It was yesterday at two fifty-four p.m.," Wendy says to Hester.

Hester nods and puts a new titanium plate over the hole in Cadmus's chest. Then out of the back pocket of her jumpsuit she pulls a sticker of a red cartoon heart and slaps it on the plate. "There. All finished."

"Will he be the same?" Damon asks her. Juni can see the hope in Damon's expression.

Hester says nothing for a moment. "The truth? I don't know. We'll have to wait and see."

Damon nods, accepting this. Juni can't bear to think of Cadmus as a basic AI but she knows she can't control what happens now.

They all stand in silence for a moment.

Finally, Drew says, "So what corp are you from, Hester? That was a serious electrical pulse in the bunker. I didn't know AI models were capable of that—knocking out power to the whole camp? That was crazy!"

Hester throws Juni a look before she answers. Juni says nothing.

"Who says I'm from a corporation?" Hester says to Drew, a sly grin on her face.

"Yeah, and is anyone gonna talk about those crazy lights? What was that about? That's the smallest tech I've ever seen," chimes in Sho.

Hester smiles. "Good question, Sho. We gotta get to the bottom of that."

CHAPTER 52

HESTER

Hester is finally starting to feel the fatigue as she enters the room where *E.T.* was shown. A makeshift hospital ward has been set up by the AI medics for the few teens who have injuries.

Sho is getting his arm put in a sling by Glykeria, who is now back to full operating capacity. He nods to Hester. Juni is sitting on a chair next to him. She is typing away on her tablet.

"Atlas won't give up, you know. There's another ship, which I'm sure they are sending our way as soon as it's repaired." Althea has entered the room. She looks even more tired than Hester.

"I know," Hester replies. "But we have time to figure out a plan."

The air is heavy as Hester wonders just how much borrowed time they have before he retaliates.

"I want to take him down, Hester. Can you and Lehmann help with that?"

Hester weighs this. The last thing she wanted was to get caught up in Earth's problems. But in her heart she knows the right answer. "You know, this wasn't really part of the plan when I first got to Earth, but he's going to kill everything good about your planet. I just can't let that happen. I'll talk to Lehmann and my boss—"

"Oh, my God, just how many bosses do you have?" says Althea, exasperated.

Hester shrugs. "It's complicated. Oh, and speaking of lunatics, where is Raze?"

Althea gestures out of the window to where *Intrepid* is docked at the end of the tunnel. "We found it a few miles away. Juni hacked into it and moved it here. Raze and all the prisoners are in the medical bay in suspension chambers, sleeping the sleep of their lives. Except Ash."

Ash.

"Where is he?" Hester asks.

"He's in Cadmus's room, with two Bobs watching over him. But he seems totally placid now, which is fascinating," Althea replies. "I'm going there now to see if he'll talk to me."

Hester nods.

"You need to tell me what those lights really are, Hester, and don't just say they're tech from your planet. I saw what they did to Ash's personality—how it looked like they snuffed the fear right out of him. I want to know how they did that. And is that what happened to Cadmus and Damon?"

Hester realizes she owes Althea. And that it will finally feel good to share the whole story with a woman she has come to trust as a friend. "OK. Let's have a terrible coffee later and we'll talk."

Althea nods. She is about to leave when she turns back to Hester. "Thank you. For helping us. You really are a remarkable girl. Wait… can I call you that?"

Hester laughs. "Sure. Suits me just fine for now."

CHAPTER 53

DREW

Later that night, Drew is in the diner with Sho. It is deserted except for the two of them and Juni, who has made them all milkshakes.

They sit there in silence, sipping, trying to process everything that has happened. They share a look with each other and then go right back to sipping, as if it's helping make sense of the last few days.

Finally, Juni looks up at Sho. "Not AI, right?"

Sho shakes his head. "Nah. You?"

"Nope."

They both look at Drew, who does nothing except sip. Then with a serious expression, they slowly start to pull their eyelid down as if to reveal metal underneath.

But they can't keep the joke up and start laughing. Juni whacks them, but she is smiling too. "Bytebrain."

"What *are* those lights?" Sho asks them. "It's like they have a mind of their own."

Drew nods. "Hester knows. We'll get it out of her."

. . .

Sho

Unable to sleep after the adrenaline of the day, Sho and Juni walk out to the forest.

They lie on the ground and stare up at the Martian sky. It's a clear night and the stars are fiercely bright against the blackness around them.

"Do you think we can make a difference back home? I want Hawkins gone so badly," Juni says.

Sho hears the quiver in her voice. It makes him realize he is desperate to see his family, but more importantly to see them free of the hell they're all living in.

He grabs her hand. "I don't know. I hope so."

Damon

It is quiet in the lab. Damon is still by Cadmus's side.

He pulls his chair closer to the table and rests his head on Cadmus's chest.

Waiting and hoping for the spark to reignite.

Hester

Hester closes the door to her room. She slumps onto her bed and stares at the ceiling, exhausted. Suddenly, she starts laughing—uncontrollable guffaws rising deep from her belly.

She knows it's just the madness of the last few days finally being released, but she still feels totally untethered.

As the peals of laughter finally calm down, Hester knows she should contact Marvin. The ship he sent for her is probably now out on the tundra, lying dormant, waiting for her own electrical signature to chart a course back to her home.

But it's not time to go home—not yet. This place has given Hester far more than she expected. She certainly didn't expect to care for it the way she does. She can't abandon Constellation, especially because her experiment is what led to where they are now. She is sure the survival of her species depends on the survival of Damon and Cadmus. But then, she also knows how important they are to the teens here.

And Atlas won't take this lying down. They need to get prepared.

Hester sits at her desk and pulls the black disc, her connection to home, from her back pocket. She stares at it for a long beat before deciding to put it in her desk drawer.

She then taps her biochip to open a screen floating in front of her. "Call Lehmann."

The screen display reads: *Calling Lehmann Industries. Connection unstable. Please hold...*

While she waits, she begins to hum to herself.

The particles of light begin to dance in front of her eyes, and she is calmed.

TIM

The TIM office is empty. It is dark, except for the glow of the large screen hovering above the desk. White noise covers the display.

An image slowly emerges through the swirling pattern of chaos. As the static fades, the scan of a brain comes into focus. The right side is human-like, but the left side is incomplete.

"File recovered. Reactivate mapping program," comes the neutral voice of TIM.

An intricate maze of lines springs forth on the screen, weaving itself into a matrix that looks very different from the right side. The matrix forms a cage-like structure, and suddenly a profusion of colors begins to flash brightly inside it.

The words, "Novel Code Detected," appear above the matrix.

"Thank you, Hester. Where there is innovation, there is revolution," says TIM.

END OF BOOK ONE.

FIND US

Thank you for going on this journey with us. Please consider leaving a review on our Amazon page: it has a big impact on the algorithm and really helps other people find this world.

And join our community:

www.aetherioncode.com
instagram.com/aetherioncodenovels

You can find Fay and Bellamy here:

instagram.com/faymastersonofficial

instagram.com/bellamyyoung
facebook.com/bellamyyoung

We hope you enjoyed Book One of The Aetherion Code trilogy. We look forward to being in touch soon!

ACKNOWLEDGMENTS

Our book would not have been possible without all these lovely people.

Katrin Van Dam gave us our first reality check on the massive holes in the initial draft. Because of her, it is pretty unrecognizable from where we began, and we will always be grateful for her incredible understanding of story and structure.

Amy Henderson, writing mentor and gifted storyteller, helped us bring out the most important elements to our story.

Erica Ellis, Corri Bell, and Halleli Abrams Gerber each shared invaluable insight into how to breathe life and authenticity into our world and its characters. Johnathan McClain was so generous with his time to help us shepherd this out into the world, instead of just leaving it in a Word file indefinitely. Eleanor Boyall truly elevated our final draft with her impressive & insightful editing skills.

We are grateful to Jason Lewis for sharing his expertise on the microscopic world that we cannot see but cannot live without, and to Andrew Dubuc for his keen eye for design. Pedro Segundo was always a loving, patient sounding board, even though science fiction is not his thing. Ira Schreck was our very earliest champion. Alissa Vradenburg has been unwavering in her support.

We deeply thank Gino Pastori-ng, Christina Cox, Linda Dubuc, Denis Dubuc, and Hannah Roberts for being our beta readers- and honest ones at that. Everyone who answered our call for advanced readers blew us away with their care & their big hearts. Extra special thanks go out to Lehlogonolo, who even at the 11th hour refined our prose, and Benji, our first online champion who utterly transformed how we brought this to the world.

Rebecca Lowman, who added more vibrancy and depth to the characters for our audiobook than we could have imagined.

Finally, to Mia, Ella, Cole, Sydney, and Sullivan: thanks for giving up precious after-school time to provide us with feedback that only teenagers can give. Sometimes only the youth can see the truth.

ABOUT THE AUTHORS

Fay Masterson is a Brit who spent thirty-odd years as an actress in film and television. She has been lucky enough to work with Tom Cruise, Jim Carrey, Stanley Kubrick, Christian Bale, and Amy Adams to name a few. She started writing screenplays in her twenties, then began tackling novels in her thirties, finally finishing one in her fifties. Better late than never. Creating this story with her brilliant friend Bellamy has been one of her proudest achievements. She hopes that her two daughters will find this book enjoyable enough that they won't mind saying their mum is one of the authors.

Bellamy Young loves animals and trying to make sense of things. A shared interest in science led her and her dear friend Fay to embark on telling this story, and every moment of that journey has been a joy. For her day job, Bellamy is best known for playing "Mellie" on ShondaLand's Scandal, but she's gotten to act extensively in television, in films from indies to blockbusters, and in theaters all the way from regional to Broadway. She grew up in Asheville, NC and graduated from Yale University. She also created the podcast She Leads with CARE and recorded the album Far Away So Close, both of which you can find on all platforms. She very much hopes you have as much fun reading The Aetherion Code as she and Fay had writing it.

www.ingramcontent.com/pod-product-compliance
Lightning Source LLC
Chambersburg PA
CBHW020409110726
47899CB00006B/1913